CRESCENDO OF FIRE

The Last Stand of the Creative Human Spirit

CRESCENDO OF FIRE

THE BRAINTRUST BOOK TWO

MARC STIEGLER

For Annette,

Marc Stiegler

April 3, 2019

LMBPN

DISRUPTIVE IMAGINATION

LMBPN Publishing
PMB 196, 2540 South Maryland Pkwy
Las Vegas, NV 89109

First US Edition, August 2018
Version 1.02, August 2018

ISBN: 978-1-64202-037-3

ACKNOWLEDGMENTS

Many people contribute to make facts behind a story true; one person, the author, is responsible for all the errors. Special thanks go to the following people for helping me right some of the wrongs in this story: Katharine McEwan, who introduced me to Jack Ainsworth and Hart Baddeley; Terry Stanley, who lent her intelligence to the birth of Dark Alpha 42; and Judith Anderle, who made the girls resplendent.

Thanks to JonLundy3d for the spaceship on the cover which was used under creative commons.

DEDICATION

For Nancy

**A Crescendo Of Fire Team Includes
JIT Beta Readers - My deepest gratitude!**

Dr. James Caplan
Erika Everest
John Ashmore
Mary Morris
Paul Westman

*If I missed anyone, **please** let me know!*

Fashion Consultant
Judith Anderle

Editor
Lynne Stiegler

FIREWORKS

People respond to incentives, although not necessarily in ways that are predictable or manifest. Therefore, one of the most powerful laws in the universe is the law of unintended consequences.

—Steven   Levitt   and   Stephen   Dubner, *SuperFreakonomics*

The clear, peaceful sky made the perfect backdrop for a beautiful explosion. The Kestrel Heavy rocket—three skyscraper-tall white cylinders strapped together, poised to launch another habitat module—gleamed in the morning sun.

The first explosions began so majestically. Huge fireballs from twenty-seven rocket engines appeared simultaneously below the craft, pushing it gracefully yet relentlessly upward. Controlled explosions these were, and all five of the people in the control room sighed with relief as she accelerated and began to tilt away to the south, over the ocean.

Then a small warning light flickered on one of the boards in the control room. A shout went up. Everyone rushed to figure out what was wrong, what to do. Too late. The computer chip dynamically controlling the fuel and oxygen flow on the port booster compensated for a thrust fluctuation a moment too late. The consequent small imbalance caused a slight twisting, which accelerated the lengthening of a microscopic fracture in one of the couplers holding the booster to the core. An instability in the airflow around the rocket wrenched the fracture into a complete break. The booster deformed from the asymmetric forces now at play along its length. The deformity ruptured the methane tank to unleash the next inferno. The fire instantly transformed into a new explosion, quite uncontrolled, that ripped through the entirety of the first stage. The whole ship flared in a blast bright enough to make the sun look dim.

From among the people watching below, silence reigned. Was this fireball intentional, somehow? Was it simply the separation of the second stage? Or had something terrible happened? Surely not.

But one person in the crowd, a gentleman so old he remembered the death of the Challenger space shuttle, knew what had happened. He pulled out his phone and called an old friend. "Colin. SpaceR just lost a ship launching from Vandenberg," he said. "They'll probably want to talk to you now. It'll take forty-eight hours or so, but they're going to be frantic when the fallout comes down. You'll be looking at a crash project, like nothing you've seen since the startup effort twenty years ago. But why am I still talking? You already know what you should do."

As he spoke, the first fallout was already making its impact felt. A helium bottle, whose contents normally regulated pressure flow from the LOX tank, hurtled free, intact and on a near-optimal trajectory to fly as far as gravity let it. Spinning on its axis with hardly a wobble, more a bullet than a tumbling piece of debris, it sailed into Los Angeles and plummeted straight into the cat's water bowl at 9080 Minerva Avenue.

The perfection of the bulls-eye would have been remarked on by neighborhood residents under any circumstances. But as it happened the young cat, a tabby with orange blotches named Marmalade, was lapping up a drink at the time. While the helium tank did not explode, its effect when it struck Marmalade was indescribably horrific. The effect on the four-year-old owner of the excessively cute fluffball was almost as bad, since she was recording the historic water-drinking event on the vidcam of her cell phone.

Although she stood far enough from the event to avoid physical harm, the little girl ceased speaking. Within the hour, the parents had decided to enter her into therapy. Long before her first session, however, her video went viral. Seventeen million views and three hours after the first round of explosions, the next series of explosions went off. These secondary blasts, political in nature, occurred in Sacramento, the capital of the Great Blue State of California.

The Governor forced his drumming fingers to still. A great opportunity had arisen here. Governors made their bones by leading forcefully in a crisis, getting out ahead of the media wave and guiding it to the desired conclusions. But risk lurked in these opportunities as well. He had this sinking feeling that it would be too easy this time to push too hard. He'd seen more than one golden goose killed in his beloved state. Worse, the memories of how GPlex and FB had responded when Federal Deportation Phase Two expelled all their immigrant engineers still sent shudders through the hierarchies of governmental power even now, decades later. The governor couldn't afford to lose any more multi-billion dollar businesses from his tax and employment base.

However concerned the governor might be, his Attorney General couldn't contain his glee. He'd been chomping at the bit for years to take these money-grubbing rocketeers down and harness them to the needs of the state. "We could never tax them as aggressively as we should have because the CEO was too damn popular," he growled.

"He is the last best example of the innovative spirit of California," the governor said dryly. "You might say he's earned it."

"Well, the kitty cat took care of that," the Attorney General replied with delight. "We can do what we want."

"What do you propose?"

"A four-billion-dollar civil forfeiture suit for public endangerment." He paused for a moment. "We can spend it immediately filling the holes in our educational and healthcare budgets."

While the amount was large enough to surprise the governor, he'd expected the Attorney General to invoke civil forfeiture. In civil forfeiture, no person or corporate entity was accused of a crime. Rather, the house, yacht, twenty-dollar bill, or in this case, the multi-billion-dollar financial account, was held accountable for illegal activity. The government never took the case to court, they just took the property regardless of the guilt or innocence of the nominal owners.

Back in the 90s, civil forfeiture had been abused so blatantly that many states had enforced limitations to keep injustice low enough to avoid headlines. But in 2017, the Federal Attorney General had announced that an inadequate number of people of unproven guilt were being targeted. He had created mechanisms to allow local law enforcement to bypass state limits.

After an initial period of slow acceptance, the states transformed into eager adopters. Civil forfeiture became the go-to legal justification for governors of both Red and Blue states. The Red governors used it simply to ruin their enemies. The Blue states used it for the more prosaic purpose of balancing their budgets.

Still, the amount of money to be taken in this instance was certainly a national record. "Four billion? Can SpaceR really survive if we take that much?" the governor asked in amazement.

"You bet they can," the Attorney General answered with a vicious undertone. "They have it now, stashed away as a rainy day fund for future R&D."

"But don't they need it for R&D? If we want them to innovate they sort of have to continue that, you know."

The Attorney General shrugged. "We'll let them keep a couple hundred mil. They can fund the rest with future profits. It'll hardly slow them down at all."

"Well, it sounds like we're finally about to get our fair share, at least. A very fair, fair share." The governor gave it some thought. It certainly sounded reasonable. "We need to pass some new regulations too, so people can feel safe again." *Get ahead of the media and stay ahead,* he repeated his mantra.

"Oh, sure." The Attorney General waved his hands and relaxed now that the governor had accepted the important part of the decision. "We'll require them to have twenty people in the control center in the future to watch for problems. Did you know they'd winnowed it down to just five? And we'll require them to retire the first-stage rockets after five uses. One of those boosters was on its twenty-first launch. Talk about a safety hazard! Damned greedy profiteers." The Attorney General knew that the mechanical part that had actually failed was only on its fourth launch and on the far side of the ship from the old booster, but factual relevance had ceased to be a consideration in government decision-making generations earlier. "If they have to make four times as many rockets, they'll have to open another assembly line in Hawthorne. Lots of jobs there."

The governor smiled. "That does sound good." He snorted. "The Feds will even like it. SpaceR launches will get more expensive. It might even let the SLS folks win a launch or two." The Space Launch System was an enormously expensive rocket project started in ancient times, back in 2011. Grossly over schedule and over budget, it had continued for decades with the support of powerful senators. It had been far too expensive to win a launch mission, but the senators had justified it "to maintain the expertise." The governor continued, "With the Feds supporting the new regulations along with us, I don't see any way it can go wrong."

A long silence ensued as the Attorney General savored the moment, and the governor thought up new things to worry about. The governor spoke hesitantly. "Still...is there anything SpaceR can *do* about it?"

The Attorney General stared at him. "Like what?"

"Could they...move their operations?"

"To where, Canada? You know the Canadians would put even more restrictions on them than we do. And there isn't another reasonable place in the USA to launch to polar orbit. Anyplace else and the rocket would fly over land. That would be seriously dangerous."

"I suppose. But..." The governor's voice fell to a frightened whisper. "What about the BrainTrust?"

The Attorney General slapped his hand on his knee and laughed loudly—perhaps too loudly. "The BrainTrust? You think they can launch from the middle of the ocean with waves ripping by all the time? Let's be real. We have a monopoly on polar orbit launch capabilities in North America. It's about time we took advantage of it."

One of the merits of living in the digital age was that

government could move very swiftly to protect the needs of the people, so less than twenty-four hours later the California Assembly passed the new laws. The little girl who had lost her kitty was only just entering therapy when the next media storm broke, carrying the word of the record-breaking civil forfeiture.

Mixed reactions greeted the news. Traditional Blues celebrated the governor's decision to get California's fair share. Stalwart believers in the human mission to space may have opposed the confiscation, but political correctness muted their response. Defending a big corporation would incur a wrathstorm on social media.

The union that controlled the workers at the SpaceR manufacturing plant in Hawthorne was ecstatic with the five-launch limit. Of course, the new regulation did not surprise them; they had lobbied for such regulations for years. Now that they had finally won, they eagerly anticipated the opening of more production lines. More union members meant more power.

No one would have been surprised to hear that less enthusiasm energized the reactions in the SpaceR boardroom. Everyone outside SpaceR figured that the fat cats would be licking their wounds and watching morosely as the state's coffers slurped up their pile of cash.

Oddly, the actual conversation at SpaceR headquarters would have surprised the general consensus. It would have astonished the governor and the Attorney General. The loss of their entire four-billion-dollar R&D fund was difficult to accept, but in the end, it was just money. They could make more.

The restriction of five launches for each rocket would

impose a frightening ongoing cost, but SpaceR could have swallowed that too. The CEO, who passionately believed in California as an operational base, certainly would have gritted his teeth and lived with the cost. But a greater problem accompanied the five launch restriction.

Far worse than the cost was the launch-capacity shortfall. They would need lots more first-stage boosters, but they could not ramp up production fast enough to replace the existing rockets before forced retirement left them dead on the launch pad. SpaceR simply could not meet their schedule with the boosters they had if rockets could not be reused as many times as they had proven safe. They would have to renege on their contracts with their customers. And that was intolerable.

The SpaceR board of directors had had a contingency in place for many years in case something terrible happened to the CEO, such as death or an intransigent refusal to face a changing reality. So the Board moved swiftly, with much personal regret but great business determination, to remove the now-not-quite-so-popular CEO and replaced him with someone considerably younger and almost as dynamic. Twenty-four hours later the new CEO's helicopter landed on the *Argus*, the ship-manufacturing vessel of the BrainTrust.

A smiling young woman escorted Matthew Toscano, the new CEO of SpaceR, and his Chief Engineer, Werner Halstead, through the ship to their meeting place. The *Argus*, like most of the isle ships, rendered the passageways of each deck with a different theme. Matt felt like hunching down when he first stepped onto the Banzai Pipeline deck. A wave off the North Shore of Oahu covered on the passage's walls and ceilings, apparently curling over his group as they walked along. The wave and a pair of surfers hanging ten as they slid through the pipe contrasted oddly with the large workspaces they passed where the latest in 3D printers hummed on diverse projects.

Eventually, Matt and company entered a small conference room with a rosewood table circled by Aeron chairs. There *Argus'* Chief Engineer Alex Turner greeted them. Alex, in turn, introduced Matt and Werner to Dr. Dash, a medical research scientist, and Colin Wheeler, who had no title.

Matt had been a wide receiver for Notre Dame while getting his degree in aerospace engineering. Fast starts off the mark and quick hands, both on and off the field, had been his trademarks—or at least that was what his wife had said when he'd asked her to marry him during her brief vacation between college cheerleading and modeling for Vogue.

Matt had thrived as an engineer, plucked from school by SpaceR when he graduated. But he found that he had an even greater talent for management than for engineering. He had hoped to do both. He could still remember the last time he had put an engineering task on the schedule for him to complete. As time passed and the project progressed, his task remained untouched. So the Friday before the Monday when his part of the project would become the critical failure in the schedule, he took a sleeping bag into the office, had his assistant manager teach him to use the current versions of the CAD and simulator software, and went to work. On Monday morning he delivered his completed task. Miraculously, he had not harmed his team or his project, but...

He had never assigned himself a task again. Instead, he rose through the ranks to his present place, depending now on Werner for technical expertise. He appraised the people. Werner appraised the tech.

At this moment, attempting to appraise the people, Matt was puzzled indeed. Alex, the Chief Engineer for the *Argus*, was a sensible person to meet. But why was a medical researcher here? And who was Colin Wheeler? He studied the tall, silver-haired gentleman—clearly quite old, but remarkably fit—and dim memories started to come back. "Colin Wheeler? The original project director for the development of the BrainTrust?" He would have sworn Colin Wheeler had passed away years ago.

Colin smiled. "That's me." He sighed. "That was a long time ago." He leaned forward. "But it was much like the problem you face now. The feds were assembling the 101st Airborne to drop into Silicon Valley and round up all the immigrant engineers. To make those jobs available for Americans, you know. But GPlex and FB didn't want to hire a whole bunch of people who were not quite as qualified and way behind the learning curve. And they sure didn't want to fire loyal employees of proven worth. So we had to rush the first couple isle ships to completion and get them out into international waters before the troops landed. It was a close thing."

Matt felt relief flow through all the hypertense muscles

in his body. He started thinking they might possibly pull this off. "And here we are again. You understand the problem?"

Colin nodded. "If you can't use your rockets more than five times you can't fulfill your contracts."

Werner spoke. "So we need to be able to launch from a ship. But the ship needs to be as robust as a standard launch facility, and just as stable. As stable as your standard isle ship may be, it is not stable enough."

Alex nodded. "We were thinking about rocket launch facilities for the BrainTrust even before your tragic accident," he confessed. "No real work, just daydreaming about it, figuring that it would be important someday. " He smiled. "Besides, it was fun." He touched his tablet, and the wallscreen behind him lit up with a photorealistic rendering of a ship, the likes of which had never before been seen. "Behold the *Heinlein*. We worked on it all night."

It was a beautiful ship in its own way. The outline followed the same rectangular, barge-like hull shape as the isle ships, but no superstructure rose from the deck except a complex metal skeleton on the starboard side amidships. Fore and aft, two solid black circles filled a large fraction of the bow and stern. A thick black line stretched from each circle to the gunwales on port and starboard sides. Clearly, the circles were launch pads, though the color was a surprise.

Werner asked the obvious question. "Are those circles just paint, or do they have some special significance?"

Alex looked sidelong at the medical scientist. "Dr. Dash, perhaps you would care to explain?" He looked back at Matt and said almost apologetically, "It was her idea."

The doctor rose to her feet and moved to the rendering of the *Heinlein*. "Thank you, Alex." Suddenly she put her hand over her mouth as a sound suspiciously like a giggle fell from her lips. "First, let me just say I am very excited by this opportunity to work with you. I have been interested in space and rocketry since I was a little girl, painting the stars in the constellations on the ceiling in my bedroom. I too have thought much about the challenges of ocean-based rocketry since I was awarded a research investment on the BrainTrust."

Matt couldn't contain himself. "A research investment in what, may I ask?"

"Telomeres," she said and turned to the display.

Matt shook his head. "Telomeres? As in the fountain of youth?"

Dash looked down at him with pursed lips. "It is most certainly *not* the fountain of youth. It is just telomeres. They do happen to play an important role in aging."

Matt nodded gravely. "Ah." He decided not to pursue the matter further.

Dash turned back to the rendering and zoomed it on the circular pad. The pad consisted of large numbers of black tiles. "These tiles are composed of a new material devised by a startup on the *Dreams Come True*, in collaboration with a professor and a student aboard the *BrainTrust University*. The new material is a variant of carbon-fiber-reinforced carbon, or CFRC. You probably know it best as the tiles for the nose of the old Space Shuttle."

Werner doubled over as if in pain. "You have got to be kidding me. Those tiles were so fragile they made the shuttle a death trap."

Dash nodded her head. "Yes. The multiple shuttle tragedies caused by tile failure tainted the material in the eyes of the public, but this is a very different application and a significantly better material. A tile failure has no dramatic consequences for the launch pad. A cracked tile merely needs to be replaced before the next launch."

She opened a small side window that displayed a complex interlace of material. "But more fundamental is the difference in the material itself. Instead of reinforcing the basic carbon matrix with carbon fiber, our people have reinforced it with graphene. Graphene Reinforced Carbon, or GRC."

Matt thought about the possible ramifications of substituting graphene, then whistled. He asked, "So it's both stronger and more heat-resistant?"

Dash bobbed her head.

Matt leaned forward suddenly like a tiger preparing to leap. "But if I recall my history correctly, those tiles were not only fragile, they were also damned expensive."

Dash nodded again. "At the time they cost a hundred thousand dollars per square foot."

Everyone gasped except Colin.

Dash continued, "A large part of the cost was the result of the extremely precise aerodynamically curved shapes required for the shuttle application. In contrast, we are simply mass-producing a standard flat hexagon. And our manufacturing techniques have advanced as well, with robotic control of the entire process. As a result of the streamlined manufacture of simple shapes, even with our more advanced and complex process using graphene, we have reduced costs to one percent of the shuttle tile costs."

Matt shook his head. "That's still pretty expensive. Why not make a normal concrete pad?"

Colin explained, "Your current pads are only normal by some very special standards. Notably, the Fondu Fyre concrete that coats the flame trench would be expensive to import here, and we can't make it. Since it ablates during each launch and needs to be replaced, this gives you both an ongoing cost and a cycle-time-to-next-launch problem. The GRC, on the other hand, has only one elemental ingredient, carbon. We manufacture carbon cheaply by harvesting and cooking algae from our artificial reef. When maintenance and replacement costs are included, I think you'll find Dash's solution is both cheaper and better."

Dash spoke. "And I think the big advantage, as Colin mentioned in passing, is the cycle time to next launch. You should be able to launch every one to two hours from a graphene-reinforced carbon pad."

Werner looked excited. "If it works, that would be magnificent."

Matt found himself distracted by applications far beyond tiling a launchpad. "Why haven't I heard of graphene-reinforced carbon before?"

Colin answered, "Many years ago, a famous actress developed a brain tumor. She claimed it was caused by graphene. The claim was controversial and the scientific evidence almost nonexistent, but on her deathbed, she was awarded four hundred million dollars. Graphene research pretty much stopped after that. Except—"

Matt finished for him, "On the BrainTrust."

Dash continued, "Anyway, to import the materials for a

classic launch pad would take about as long as manufacturing the tiles—which brings up an issue. The tiles must be steeped in a carbon-rich vapor. Think of it as a curing process. It will take us a week to make the tiles, and a day to place them. Can you wait that long?"

Matt blinked. "You think you can start launching in a week? What about building the ship that needs to go underneath those launch pads?"

Alex supplied the answer. "We have a partly-completed isle ship currently under construction. We had intended to make it into the manufacturing ship for the Fuxing archipelago. We can repurpose the ship, and build another ship for the Fuxing project."

Matt knew what was coming. "For a satisfactory fee."

Alex nodded. "We've assumed that time is more important than cost for you, within limits."

Matt laughed playfully. Everyone understood that Matt would fight tooth and nail over the costs of the more outrageous line items, but for now… "Price is no object. It's so freeing, isn't it, to unshackle yourself from the constant grinding need to reduce costs?" He turned sober. "You do realize we have a little financing problem as well? The four billion in liquid assets we had two days ago is going away."

Colin leaned forward. "We're aware. And to fulfill your needs on a crash-project timeline, it looks like we're talking about a two-billion-dollar undertaking here. But there are several financing alternatives." He held up his phone. "I have representatives from both the Goldman Sachs and JP Morgan offices here on the BrainTrust sitting outside eager to talk with you about some possibilities." He rolled his eyes as he reluctantly added another option. "And in a few days the new isle ship *Haven*, a residential ship built and populated by billionaires, will arrive. You could probably make a deal with their consortium." He grimaced. "I would be careful with them, however."

Matt laughed again. "And I don't have to be careful with the boys and girls from Goldman?" He expression turned speculative. "Are you really sure you can be ready to launch in a week?"

Alex shrugged. "Ten days," he admitted cautiously. "No more than that, if you give me the go-ahead today."

Matt shook his head. "I can't possibly get the finances all lined up in time."

Colin waved it aside. "We don't need the finances all fixed to begin work. You have an excellent reputation, Matthew Toscano. We just need your handshake. We'll take the risk that your word is good."

Werner growled, "We still haven't talked stability."

Alex answered, "I think you'll be pleasantly surprised."

Werner looked skeptical.

Matt leaned forward and thumped the table. "Werner, you stay here and talk stability." He looked at Colin. "Is there a private place—a very private place—where I can talk to the Goldman rep? I have an idea." His face had turned hard and angry, but a hint of a smile now played on his lips. "A very satisfying idea, actually. Let justice be served." He clenched his fist and released it. "Werner, if you get an adequate answer on the ship, and I get an adequate idea on the money, we'll see if we can kick this plan off by dinnertime."

So Colin introduced Matt to Keenan Stull of Goldman Sachs, and Alex and Dash talked with Werner, and many hurdles were identified and overcome, at least on paper. And so when Alex met Werner and Matt for dinner, the real work began.

Half-empty champagne glasses sat on the desk in the office of the President of the Russian Union, seeming to glow in the setting sun's light. Pascha gazed into the mirror in the lid of her compact and fixed her lipstick. The President buckled his pants.

Except I am no longer President, he reminded himself as he picked up the champagne flute for another sip in self-congratulation. He was now the Premier of the Russian Union. No more pesky elections. The Premiership was a lifetime post. He had certainly earned it.

Now that he had finally freed up all the time he used to spend managing the electoral cycle, destroying his dangerously popular opponents, setting up dummy candidates as alternatives on the ballots, and making sure the news media toed the line, he could focus on wielding that power fulltime rather than just half.

It was time to take the matter of getting old seriously. He was having trouble giving Pascha all the satisfaction she deserved.

Judging by his last, admittedly hasty effort to retrieve the rejuvenation doctor from the BrainTrust, he needed a more serious plan this time—even if it meant blowing the cover on one of his top assets.

2

COUNTING DOWN

Life is all about picking yourself up over and over again.
   —Lindsey Stirling

The entire BrainTrust, it seemed, turned out 24/7 for the task of getting the *Heinlein* ready for launch. The students on the *BTU* turned out full-force, producing final detailed plans for the different parts of the ship or programming the bots to implement those plans or just wrangling the bots in real-time to account for programming and planning deficiencies.

Almost all were motivated to participate to a greater or lesser extent by knowing that this project had a rendezvous with destiny. They knew they wanted to be able to tell the story. "I was there, and this is how I helped make history happen."

But there were other motivations as well. Some of the politically enthusiastic students— the Reds and the Libertarians—loved the opportunity to poke the Blue California government in the eye. Others came because their friends had urged them to. Still others saw the girls they wanted to date (but were afraid to ask) helping, so they joined to get the chance to talk to the girls.

And of course, most were motivated to some degree by the whopping bonuses if they finished on time—in ten days.

Matt watched the expenses accumulate at an incredible rate and shook his head. He calmed himself by looking through his virtual window on the *Elysian Fields*, watching as his new ship practically leaped into existence at a rate he also found incredible. Werner, who didn't care about the cost, glowed with elation as he stood in the thick of things on the *Heinlein*, supervising everything he could get his eyes on. Periodically Alex or Colin would go out and distract him to help the workers get their tasks done.

The professors were at least as engaged as the students, so for ten days the *BTU* effectively closed its doors. Even the med students turned out, because somehow, even though all the hands-on labor was being done by bots, the students and professors and even the professional ship engineers still managed to get themselves injured.

Virtually all the startup companies on the *Dreams Come True* ceased normal operations as well. Each of them had a mad new tech, and somehow each and every last one of their CEOs could easily explain why their latest invention was the critical new piece of gear needed for seaborne rocket launch.

Matt looked at the gaggle of tech magicians in dismay, but soon enough figured out that Dash was the perfect person to filter out the noise. She knew all the new technologies under development, and she understood the core needs of the project. She understood Matt's greatest concern. "I understand, Mr. Toscano. It is not a problem if it is a little expensive, but it is a disaster if there is a little risk."

At first, Matt wondered how many lifelong enemies Dash was making in the startup companies. He could see no way she could get the respect she needed from them to accept her decisions as final. He eventually concluded his concerns had been naive. The CEOs seemed a little afraid of her, while the tech leads tended to look at her in awe. He soon learned her full name. She was known on the *Dreams Come True* as Doctor *"I believe this can be improved upon"* Dash. In the end, he thanked Alex for sending her to him. She was saving his life, he explained. Alex grunted. "She does that sometimes," was all he would say.

Housing was a problem. The *Elysian Fields* had nearly full booking; Matt was lucky indeed to get himself a single cabin. But the *Heinlein's* launch facilities needed the expertise of Matt's best and brightest from his launch crew, so even though Matt had brought less than half his personnel from Vandenberg, the archipelago had no place for any of them to stay. Colin and Amanda—the current Chairman of the Board for the BrainTrust—encouraged the residents of all the ships to run a variant of an Airbnb, renting out beds rather than rooms, no residents having a whole spare room due to BrainTrust policies. Naturally, in keeping with their entrepreneurial spirit, the residents charged exorbitant prices for these beds. Matt just sighed and paid.

Eight days from First Launch, the *Haven* showed up and cut a deal to dock off the *Dreams Come True*. The *Haven* was a purely residential ship, built by a consortium of billionaires so they could have homes larger than the single-cabin dwellings standard throughout the BrainTrust. The *Haven* arrived expecting to be the center of attention and much fanfare, bringing many of the rich and famous with much capital for investments in BrainTrust enterprises. No one noticed them.

When the *Haven* residents found out that the advent of SpaceR had completely overshadowed their own arrival, rocket fever infected them as well. They immediately set to work figuring out how they could exploit the upcoming event.

Seven nights before First Launch, at midnight, three of SpaceR's four Autonomous SpacePort Drone Ships made port in San Pedro. SpaceR workers moving quietly, swiftly, and in near darkness, loaded each drone with four side boosters and two cores, enough for two heavy-launch rockets per drone ship. Those six rockets would be the Polar Orbit fleet for SpaceR for the next several months.

The drones had not been designed to carry so many boosters; they'd had to be modified to accomplish it. Having six boosters loaded on a platform designed for a one-booster landing was precarious at best, but in the end, SpaceR's team had the boosters locked down and ready to sail. The drones left port again before the sun rose; before either the media or the California government learned of either the drones' departure or their precious cargo.

Six days and counting, near noon, Dash stood by Matt on

the topmost deck (the roof) of the *FB Alpha* watching as the rockets on their drones glided across surprisingly calm waters. Dash had invited him here to watch the drones arrive. It was one of her favorite places since most of the deck was a lush botanical garden that included plants from all over the world, including Dash's home in Bali.

Dash frowned. "Are you sure you had to take your own rockets like a thief in the night?"

Matt replied curtly, "Don't know, don't want to find out. What good could come of it if the politicians found out? Think they'd apologize, tell us to keep our money, and offer us drinks on the house if we came back?"

Dash shook her head. "You know they'll find out in a day or so. Someone involved with loading the rockets is bound to Twitter about it."

Matt shrugged. "The later, the better." He pointed farther to the east. "See those California Coastal Patrol ships? Above all things, I want to get those rockets docked here before they decide they're supposed to do something."

Time compressed. Shortcuts were taken. Only one of the two launch pads was properly outfitted with reinforced carbon. The other was temporarily covered in Portland cement, adequate to withstand the relatively small shock of the landing of a single booster but not the launch of a full heavy rocket.

With five days left, a key part of the plan had to be scratched and revamped. One of the projects Dash had cautiously recommended to Matt for funding was a prototype algae-to-methane converter for making the fuel. It would be very cheap and efficient, if the inventors could only get it to work for more than fifteen minutes before clogging up. On this fifth day, Dash told Matt it wouldn't be ready in time, no matter what the CEO and tech lead might say.

Dash said not to worry, that she had a contingency. She had Matt contact the operators of all the ships in the BrainTrust.

The tiny fish-oil-to-diesel converters found on every isle ship, used to supply fuel for their small numbers of non-electric vehicles, could be temporarily converted—for a price—with minor modifications and a substantial loss of efficiency, to make methane instead. By the end of the day, hastily-converted robo-vans were carting loads of methane from throughout the BrainTrust to the *Heinlein*. The *Heinlein* chilled the fuel and stored it in new tanks on the lower decks.

Once that effort was in operation, Matt started calling shipping operators around the globe to find an LNG tanker he could lease and fill with methane. They would not need it for First Launch, but they would certainly need it soon.

Meanwhile, liquid oxygen generators were tested aboard the *Heinlein*, not to be used for real until launch day, when they would directly load the rocket's LOX tanks. The LOX generator was powered by the *Heinlein's* nuclear reactors, only one of which was currently operational. But one reactor would be enough for First Launch.

Four days remained. The Vehicle Assembler and Transporter Tower, the complex titanium skeleton Matt had first seen depicted in the renderings of the *Heinlein* on his first day on the BrainTrust, came together from a parts run off the 3D printers on the *Argus*. In the first test of the VATT's ability to lift a booster from the drone platform onto the *Heinlein*, the cylinder swayed, struck the *Heinlein* starboard amidships, and crashed to a watery grave.

Matt's heart skipped three beats as he watched the graceful disaster from a perch on the *Argus*. "I can't… I don't know…"

Werner crumpled beside him. "How?"

Colin visibly straightened as if preparing for gladiatorial combat. Matt was suspicious that Dash and Colin had started taking turns babysitting the top SpaceR management, i.e., Werner and him, as the days counted down and the ability of upper management to positively impact operations receded into the sunset.

But today Dash had actually returned to her office for a little while, "to get some real work done." She'd apparently left Colin with the babysitting duty for this event.

Colin smiled. "Cheer up, folks," he offered brightly. "Aren't you glad that was just a mockup booster, not a real one? Do you think our people decided to use the mockup first because they were certain it would all work right the first time? Of course not. Our teams expected this." Honesty compelled him to soften his claim. "Well, they didn't really expect it, but they prepared for it. Contingency plans are already in motion."

Colin held his finger up as if to point triumphantly as

said plans went into effect, but hastily put his hand back down. The VATT crew was looking forlornly over the side of the ship at the hull dent, as uncertain what to do as Matt and Werner. "At the team-management level, of course. Contingency plans. In motion."

All three of them watched, paralyzed, as nothing happened.

Then Alex ran onto the *Heinlein's* deck and started shouting orders.

Matt could hear Colin exhale his held breath. "See?"

Three days left. It was the seventh day of the effort. And on the seventh day...no one rested.

However, a couple of people who thought they were akin to God rose up in righteous wrath.

The governor sat rigid in his chair, watching a disaster unfold before him on the wallscreen. He watched the scene over and over again, transfixed by horror. It was a YouTube video, very poor quality, captured with a cell phone at 2AM in the Port of Los Angeles at San Pedro. It showed three rocket-lander drone ships departing the docks with a virtual forest of skyscraper-tall rocket boosters on board.

Occasionally, the governor would break the cyclic rhythm of the replay to show a companion video taken in bright daylight of a booster being lifted up the side of a modified isle ship. The drones with the forest of boosters could be seen in the background. He held his breath every time the booster being lifted crashed back into the sea. "What were they thinking?" he half-screamed to himself. "Has the new CEO of SpaceR gone mad?"

The Attorney General was staring down at his own laptop, completely oblivious to the comings and goings of boosters on the sea. Something far more terrible had happened. "Those greedy, selfish bastards," he muttered. "Greedy. Selfish. *Bastards!*"

The governor tore his eyes away from the wallscreen. "They don't look greedy from here. They look like idiots."

The Attorney General jerked his hand in a brush-off that wanted to be a smack-down of someone's face. "I'm not talking about the rockets. Forget the rockets. I'm talking about the money!"

The governor blinked at him in confusion. "The money? What about the money?"

"They stole it!" The Attorney General jerked back in his seat and glared at the governor. "When we first contacted SpaceR, they promised they'd authorize the transfer of the four billion within forty-eight hours, but then they appointed the new CEO. He transferred the money to Goldman Sachs, claiming it would be easier for them to convert such large investments into cash. He explained he didn't want us to suffer any losses from a crash in the value of the bonds." The Attorney General spat, "From that moment on, Goldman started giving us the runaround. Oh, we need an extra day to dissolve the holdings. Oh, the transfer authentication number is incorrect. Oh, we need authorization from one of the partners. Oops, the account accidentally got sent to the Caymans. We'll get it back. On and on." He took a deep breath. "Now we're locked out. No one is answering my calls. I just get an admin who keeps apologizing and promising her boss will get back to us as soon as possible."

The governor shrugged. "So get a court order."

The Attorney General shook his head. "They moved the money onto the BrainTrust. You know Goldman Sachs has two isle ships there, right?"

The governor's voice fell. "The BrainTrust. Again."

The Attorney General ran both his hands through his hair. "They'll pay for this. We'll punish them for it. We just have to figure out how."

The governor watched the booster crash into the sea again. "It may be pretty simple, actually."

Day Eight. The VATT lifted the parts of a mockup rocket, assembled them, and trundled the resulting vehicle over to the launch pad. After a few tests, the VATT then started to transport the rocket back to the side for offloading. As the machine crossed the edge of the pad, where the graphene reinforced carbon met the surrounding cement, it died.

Colin, Dash, and Matt watched from the roof deck of the *Argus* as the VATT shuddered to a stop. Matt groaned.

Colin shook his head. "You need more Zen in your life, Matt. Looks like it got hung up on the edge of the pad. This is just a passing glitch."

People and machines swarmed over the structure, then as quickly ran from it. The VATT started moving again.

"See," Colin continued, "No problem. Forty bots, twenty grad students, five engineers, and a partridge in a pear tree were able to get it moving again in moments."

Matt looked at the sky. "I think the partridge made the difference." He nodded his head sharply. "Good enough. It may all be rickety, but it's going to work. Time to stop playing games with the Glorious State of California. I'll tell Keenan to tell them they aren't getting our money, though I imagine they already suspect that."

Dash left shortly thereafter to make a visit to her lab. She, like everyone else, was taking a ten-day break in her normal routine to support the launch effort. She hadn't been back to the lab since Matt had arrived. Truthfully, she'd been putting off going back. She had enjoyed working with Byron so much, but it had ended so badly. Without an intern, the lab was, honestly, a little bit lonely. Still, there were things to do, and she should do some of them.

Meanwhile, on Minerva Avenue, a little girl's father took her into their backyard and showed her his own engineering project. He had built a roof to go over the cat food dishes. He told her the roof was very strong and set her atop it to demonstrate that. She still looked doubtful, so he climbed up on the roof with her, wrapped his knuckles on the shingles, and promised no rocket could get through. This seemed to calm her.

Together they slid underneath the roof and sat by the water bowl. Her mother then came out, carrying a tiny black and white kitty, and handed it to the little girl. Mom said the kitty's name was Fluffy, and the father demonstrated great wisdom by not pointing out that the kitten was so thin it would be better named "Skinny." The kitty purred as the little girl stroked her ears.

On the ninth day, the VATT hoisted the first-stage boosters and the second stage and the payload onto the deck. The VATT assembled them and wheeled them onto the pad. A short firing test was conducted. Meanwhile, the isle ships of the BrainTrust disconnected their network of gangways, and all the ships moved out to form a loose ring about a mile away from the *Heinlein*. Matt watched the fleet evolution from the *Argus*, standing by the gunwales on the port side, letting the cold ocean breeze whip against his face. Dash and Colin were with him. Werner and Alex were still aboard the *Heinlein*, making sure everything was ready.

Matt's anxiety level had been rising constantly as they got closer to the launch. He clenched his teeth against the chill and clenched his hands against the winds of fate. "They're still too close," he complained again. "We could wipe out half the BrainTrust if this goes badly."

Dash put a reassuring hand on his forearm. "This was the agreement we reached with Werner. We didn't have enough time to acquire the gyroscopic stabilizers for the hull, so for these first couple of launches, the ships of the BrainTrust will act as a wall around the *Heinlein* to dampen the wind and waves." She blew out a frustrated breath. "I personally think it's an unnecessary precaution. It's not like we're going to launch in the middle of a typhoon, and the Sea Launch Corporation was doing such launches from a repurposed offshore oil-drilling platform in 1999. But we all agreed."

Colin added, "And you're a little over-concerned. I think you'd find that the isle ships are reasonably robust even in the face of a catastrophic explosion." He paused, then confessed, "Well, the older ones are. The newest ships might go up rather spectacularly if the explosion breached the titanium coatings on the superstructure and the flames lit the underlying magnesium, but that's really unlikely."

"*Way* too close," Matt muttered. "We should at least evacuate the people."

Colin answered, "We've offered ferry rides to anyone who's interested in being farther away. I think you'd be surprised by how few people are taking us up on the offer. The launch is the talk of the whole fleet. Everybody wants to see what we've wrought—what *they* have wrought for the future of space flight."

"Umph." Matt turned and walked back inside the ship.

Back in California, the little girl opened her mouth several times as if to speak. The psychologist was very excited.

Dash had gotten close enough to see *Bu* Amanda waiting for her in her office when she heard her name shouted from down the passageway. She turned and waved. "Ben! Good to see you."

Honestly, it was not as good as it might have been to see him. Ben had been one of her patients in her first anti-aging trials using telomere therapy. Unlike all the other patients, it had neither given him a new lease on life nor killed him outright. At the time of the trials, he had walked haltingly but unaided. Now he came toward her using a walker. He was hunched over and worn-looking. Dash was at least glad to see that when he reached her, he straightened up from the walker and breathed normally. His smile still shone brightly. "Whatever you do, don't tell me I'm looking young for my age."

Dash just shook her head and returned his smile. "What are you doing here? We do not have any more checkups scheduled. Is there something amiss?"

He laughed. He was always laughing; it was almost unnerving. "No, something wonderful is happening, and I came looking for you to invite you to the celebration."

Dash responded with the topmost thing in her mind. "First Launch is tomorrow! Of course." She paused, puzzled. "Celebration?"

Ben spread his arms wide, swaying slightly without the support of the walker. "Celebration! You know the *Haven* has arrived, right?"

Dash nodded.

"And I told you long ago that I had a pad on board, though I was planning to stay in my cabin on the *Dreams Come True* and rent out my *Haven* place."

Dash nodded again.

"So, the whole *Haven* is turning itself into a party boat

for a pre-launch party. My pad is going to be ground zero for the event." He put his hand on her shoulder. "You're invited. I won't take no for an answer. You simply have to be one of my guests. You're the talk of the ship, you know. Everyone wants to meet you."

Dash looked away with a mild frown. "I am sorry, Ben, but I was hoping to watch the launch with friends. Other friends, that is," she added for clarification.

"So bring them along. Just who all were you going to watch with?"

Dash shifted her head side to side. "Well, we have been so busy we have not really talked about a plan yet —"

"Excellent."

"But I was expecting to watch the launch with Matt Toscano —"

"CEO of SpaceR?!" Ben's eyes widened.

Dash did not notice his surprise. "*Pak* Colin —"

Ben chortled. "Wheeler! Why am I not surprised?"

"And probably *Bu* Amanda —"

"Chairman of the Board of the BrainTrust! Perfect! No wonder none of them have RSVP'd my invitations; they're all planning to hang out with you! Girl, you have a more high-octane power-brokering party planned than I do. You must bring them to my place. I guarantee you'll enjoy it. My place on the *Haven* simply must be seen to be believed."

Dash looked skeptical. "I suppose it sounds as if I have been collecting, what would you call them, 'movers and shakers,' but that really wasn't my plan."

Ben's laughter this time started in his chest and shook his whole body, and he wheezed as he took his next breath. "Of course not, Dash, I never thought it at all."

"But not everyone I was hoping to share the launch with is a mover or a shaker. I was also hoping to be with my best friends, Ping and Jam. They are just peacekeepers."

Ben blinked at her. "'Just peacekeepers.' Is that what you think? They're the pair who took out the loony-tune Blue who tried to kill you, right?"

Dash nodded again. "And Colin. They saved Colin, too."

Ben started to laugh again, but a wave of pain passed over his face, and he stopped. "Ping and Jam, the two heroes of Assault Night, and you call them 'just peace-keepers.'"

Dash stomped her foot softly. "No, I do *not* call them 'just peacekeepers.' I call them my friends."

Ben hid his face in his hands. "Girl, they are just as famous as you are, at least here on the BrainTrust." He put his hands down and looked at her thoughtfully. For the first time in the conversation, he did not look like he was going to laugh. "Even if they were not famous, they would still be welcome at our *Haven* party. Simply because they are your friends, for one thing." He twitched his nose. "But there's more to it than that. I'm sure at this point you've got the impression that my goal is to have the most presti-gious party with the most powerful people around as my guests. You probably think I want 'everybody who is anybody' to come, right?"

Dash shrugged. "It certainly sounds like it."

Ben shook his head. "And that is true as far as it goes. But they are the second-most-desired guests when I throw a party. There's a group that I want to invite even more, though they are much harder to find." He raised an eyebrow at her.

Dash rolled her eyes. "Do not make me guess, for I do not know. Who do you most wish to attend your parties?"

"The people who are not yet anybody, but who will definitely be, at some future time, somebody." A dreamy look came to his eyes. "There's nothing quite like having a photo, fifty years down the road, showing that 'I knew her way back when, before she was famous.'" He looked back at Dash. "Even if Ping and Jam were not already famous, if they were just your friends, they would probably be destined for great things."

He shook his finger at her. "You lift the people around you up. You can't help it. Mark my words: someday Ping and Jam will be known far beyond the confines of the BrainTrust archipelago." He paused, and a pleading note entered his voice. "Come to my party. Bring anyone you want. Please."

Dash sighed. He was not making this easy for her. Worse, perhaps he was right. She was about to say she'd think about it when another voice came from behind her.

"Dash, he's right. You should go," Amanda confirmed as she came down the hall from Dash's office. She looked at Ben. "I couldn't help hearing. Your voice carries, you know. Sort of like a moose calling."

Ben laughed once more.

Amanda looked back at Dash. "He really *will* have the movers and the shakers of the world there. You need to meet them." She paused, clearly wishing she didn't have to continue but driven by honesty. "You're one of them now."

Ben interrupted, "*Us*, Amanda. She's one of *us* now. Do not pretend you're not one."

"Us," Amanda conceded. She smiled. "It's not everyone

who's so important that the Chief Advisor of the United States tries to kidnap them."

More laughter from Ben. "Yes, that's an honor most of my guests haven't yet had." He scrunched his face in thought. "Though from what I hear, at least the governor of California would like to kidnap Matthew at this point." He grasped the handles of his walker and twisted about, then looked over his shoulder. "Cocktail party. Ties, no tails. Launch at noon, party starts at 9AM," he relayed, then scooted off with surprising speed to capture his next guest.

Dash's shoulders slumped. "He is so jovial. I am always exhausted when we finally finish speaking."

Amanda started laughing at this, then she turned serious. "Dash, do you have a proper cocktail dress for a billionaire's party at a billionaire's mansion?"

Dash frowned. "I hardly think he has a mansion on the *Haven*. He says he has a 'cozy pad.'"

Amanda shook her head. "Trust me. Do you have a dress?"

Dash answered doubtfully, "Yes. At least, I think so."

"And Jam and Ping?"

Dash sighed. "Probably not."

"Then we have a problem."

Dash was pleased that *Bu* Amanda viewed it as her problem too.

Amanda, showing a touch of telepathy, explained, "You'll all be representing the residents of the *Chiron*. You must not let anyone outshine you." Her eyes gleamed momentarily. "*You* must outshine *everyone*."

Amanda started tapping on her tablet, frowning from time to time. She growled, "I just hate it when those people make us dance to their tune." She looked up at Dash. "We have some very fine boutiques throughout the BrainTrust, but none of them up to the standard that the *Haven* brought with them. You'll all need dresses from Sea Change, which is on the *Haven* promenade."

Amanda sent email to Jam and Ping, demanding, in her role as their boss, that they meet Amanda and Dash at the shop at 5PM sharp. "This is going to be an emergency rush job, just like the *Heinlein*. They're going to charge us through the nose to have your dresses ready by morning."

Dash approached the entrance to the Sea Change. The storefront seemed too narrow to house an actual boutique. The door, framed in rococo swirls of gold, was flanked by two windows just wide enough for one full-length narrow-skirted dress apiece.

Jam, Ping, and Amanda awaited her. "Sorry," she mumbled. "Got tied up." All three of her companions frowned. *Of course, you did*, their eyes said eloquently. Dash straightened her shoulders and marched forward.

A middle-aged woman with short, straight black hair hustled up to them. Dash suspected she might have been even shorter than she was, but she moved atop impossibly high platform heels. Dash suppressed a flicker of irritation. It would be nice, just once, to be at eye-level with someone besides Ping. "Good evening. I'm Daniella," she greeted them with a gracious smile and quick, clipped words.

Amanda explained the crisis. "These three need outstanding outfits for Ben Wilson's party tomorrow. I'm thinking, we will need Tory Burch, definitely Chanel or Prada, and of course, Versace for Ping." She pointed at her tallest companion. "Jam will need something conservative, yet stunning." At the moment Jam wore her peacekeeper's uniform: black pants, a yellow shirt, and a black scarf over her head.

Daniella nodded. "Pakistani? It will be a delight working with you. I get so few Pakistani clients here, you know."

Jam raised an eyebrow. "I'm surprised you get *any*."

Amanda pointed again. "This is Ping." Ping had come dressed in short shorts and a tank top that showed off her tattoos. It looked a great deal like the outfit she'd worn to take down Jam's brother-in-law, who'd come with Jam's ex-husband to conduct an honor killing.

Daniella had apparently heard about that incident. "Ah, of course. Ping the hooker who also is a peacekeeper." As everyone stared at her, she chuckled. "Oh, yes, we've heard about you. Half the residents are interested in Dr. Dash's rejuvenation therapy, and we're all thankful you saved her on Assault Night." She turned back to Jam as she realized who her new Pakistani client was. "And you too." She looked at Ping critically, running a finger lightly down the phoenix inked on her left arm. "For anyone else with tattoos I'd recommend long sleeves for a formal party, but you? *Definitely* strapless."

Amanda pointed at Dash but was too late for the introduction. Daniella clasped her hands together delightedly. "And you simply *must* be Dr. Dash. I'm so *thrilled* to make your acquaintance."

Dash wanted to shrink out the door but knew Amanda

wouldn't allow it. "Call me Dash," she said softly, "Just Dash."

Daniella nodded. "Dash. Amanda's right. Tory Burch." She paused. "You know you'll, uh…"

Amanda completed the sentence, "Dash, ditch the lab coat. She needs to be able to see you."

Daniella looked relieved. "Yes, exactly."

Dash looked around the small room, bewildered. "You have no dresses here. How can we try on—"

Daniella stepped away and gestured at the walls, which responded immediately. On each wall, a different model appeared, one each of Dash, Jam, and Ping. Daniella spoke again, once to each wall, and the three likenesses of her clients acquired dresses immediately recognizable as too expensive for any sane person to purchase.

Dash swallowed. "Never mind."

Daniella kept up a running stream of analysis as she discussed with Amanda the best choices for each of them. In those rare moments when Dash, Jam, and Ping got a word in edgewise, Amanda and Daniella acted as if they had not heard. As if the people at the center of this process were too ignorant to offer a useful opinion, which, as Dash ruefully acknowledged to herself, was probably correct.

In the end, Daniella and Amanda confessed to being fully satisfied with the outcome. For Dash, Daniella had found Tory Burch's Evaline Cold Shoulder dress with tassels in white and a pair of Prada's kitten heels in the pink and silver to provide a hint of color.

Jam, after an hour of soul-searching, found her virtual self in a Chanel, one of the latest ensembles by Karl Lagerfeld shown during the Chanel Ready-to-Wear

Spring/Summer Show. The tweed-ink, blue, and ecru one-piece showed off her height. Danielle had paired the dress with Chanel's classic spectators in black and white.

Ping, meanwhile, had settled upon a Versace strapless, a fully beaded thigh-length...covered in Warhol icons. Dolce & Gabbana embroidered velvet pumps and a pair of diamond chandelier earrings topped off the chic gaudiness of it all.

At which point Dash looked at Jam, who was looking longingly at the dress chosen for her, while Ping stared at her image in a way that made Dash look more closely at her to see if steam really was coming out of her ears. Dash realized she had to speak for all three of them. "Daniella, *Bu* Amanda, we all appreciate what you're trying to do for us, but really, none of us can afford these dresses."

Amanda looked at her in astonishment. "You...you can't afford it?" She peered hard into Dash's eyes. "What have you been spending all your bonuses on?"

Dash looked at her in puzzlement that slowly faded. "Bonuses? You mean from the successful rejuvenations?"

Amanda's expression turned into a glare. "Yes, of course. The bonuses."

Dash blinked. "Well, I, ah, I've been really busy."

Jam tore her eyes away from the dress she could not have. "Let me guess. You've never looked at your bonuses. You have no idea how much money you have."

Dash grimaced. "As project lead, my room and board are paid for automatically. I hardly need any money." She pointed at the lab coat they had forced her to discard so the boutique's computers could get her measurements. "Well, I bought a new lab coat. That's about it."

Amanda put her hand to her temples and rubbed them. "Dash, would you please look at your bonus account?"

Dash grumbled as she worked her tablet and her eyes widened. "Oh. Goodness." She looked up at Amanda. "I guess I can afford it after all."

Amanda gave her a smug smile. "And you'll probably have enough left over to buy a stick of gum, too."

Millions of sticks of gum, Dash realized. Then her heart sank as she realized, looking at Jam and Ping, that her sudden rise to riches solved only one-third of the problem. She certainly had enough money to solve the whole problem, but how? If she offered to pay for the outfits, Jam and Ping would probably refuse outright.

She looked at Amanda, who looked back mischievously and then turned to Daniella. "Could Dash and I speak with you in the back for a moment?"

Jam and Ping watched them suspiciously as they departed. They returned, having agreed to Amanda's plan quickly—before Jam and Ping got so worried they tried eavesdropping.

Daniella clapped her hands. "I don't normally do this, but as Dash and Amanda just pointed out to me, you two are so famous you'll make great advertisements for my styles. I can let you rent the dresses for a day." She named a price comparable to that of a new pair of blue jeans.

Jam gawked. "But...the dresses are useless to anyone else, right? They're custom-tailored to our measurements, aren't they?"

Daniella waved the question away airily. "Of course. Of course, I have to get right to work immediately to meet your schedule for tomorrow morning—9AM is the party, right?"

Jam nodded.

"Well, then, the dresses should be fine." She gestured to the walls once more, and the images of the two peace-keepers and the medical researcher disappeared. In their stead, a set of mirrors arose. "The dresses are printing as we speak. You'll need to come in for a final fitting at 7AM. Now, about the jewelry…"

Dash was sure she looked as shell-shocked as Jam, though Ping just scowled.

A bot rolled into the room with three cases. Daniella opened the first one. "For Dash," she announced and wrapped an Enticelle De Cartier necklace made of white gold and diamonds around her neck. Dash put on the earrings made of platinum, emeralds, onyx, and diamonds. Daniella held up the Panthere De Cartier Brooch made of white gold, emeralds, onyx, and diamonds so Dash could see the entire suite of jewelry. The mirrors reflected the glory of the gems, and Dash gasped.

Daniella's eyes gleamed triumphantly. "Yes, that'll do." She opened the next container, pulling out a Pearl necklace from Mikimoto which turned out to be two necklaces in one. The shorter one with two diamond-encrusted pendants and the longer strand all in pearls glowed with soft resplendence, falling from Jam's shoulders.

Jam opened her mouth to object, but Dash spoke first. "Perfect. It's perfect as a housewarming gift."

Jam stared at her.

Dash put her hands on her hips. "*You* gave *me* a housewarming gift, you know—that beautiful rug in my office. I know it cost you everything you had. This is yours."

Amanda also spoke before Jam could utter a word. "Jam, say thank you, and accept graciously. You really have no choice."

Jam paused, spun to look at herself in all the mirrors, and acquiesced. "Thank you, Dash."

Daniella reached for the third case, but Ping held up her hand. "Hold it." She blew out a sharp breath. "I've got this covered." She squeezed her hand into the taut pocket of her shorts and pulled forth a long string of diamonds.

Daniella leaned over to examine the necklace more closely and gasped. "A Vivienne." Her eyes widened. "From the 20s. How did... Where did you..." She straightened and looked quizzically at Ping. "That will work."

"Yeah, yeah, yeah. Long story," Ping dodged the question everyone wanted to ask while jamming the diamonds back in her pocket with an urgency that suggested she just wanted them to disappear.

Daniella blinked. "Well, I'll expect you all again at 7AM." Her voice turned stern. "Don't be late."

They had barely escaped the boutique when Ping rounded on Dash and whispered in her ear, "If you bought those dresses for us on the sly and had Daniella go along with this little charade, I'll...I'll...I'll have to squeeze you to death." At which point she squeezed Dash, not quite to death. "But you still owe me a housewarming present. You got Jam those beautiful jewels. That's fine, but I want something *really* special. I'll let you know when I find it."

Dash tried and failed to guess what would possibly make a good housewarming present for Ping. She had a terrible feeling she would eventually find out.

3

FIRST LAUNCH

The best way to predict the future is to create it.
 —Alan Kay, 1971

"Starships were meant to fly" were the first words Dash heard on crossing the threshold into Ben's cozy pad on the *Haven*, the words of a song playing softly in the background.

Ping gave a sigh of satisfaction. "Nikki Minaj. An oldie but a goodie. Who'd have thought a creaky old geezer like Ben Wilson would have good taste in music?"

Jam swept the enormous room with her eyes. "Are all these people really billionaires? I never would have guessed there could be so many." She pointed to the right, seemingly at the ornate ebony-wood bar where two older men sat on stools, discussing either the implications of the hyperinflationary phase of the birth of the universe or the best stocks in their portfolios. "I didn't expect them to be that young, either."

Dash raised an eyebrow. "Those two gentlemen do not look all that young to me."

Jam waved her finger again. "Not them. The ones on the dance floor, silly."

Dash shifted her gaze slightly to a small cluster of young people, college-age at best, dancing on a makeshift platform by the bar. "Ah." She thought about it for a moment. "They could actually be billionaires, you know, it happens here. But they are more likely to be the children of billionaires. We could ask, I suppose."

Ben's voice washed over them from nearby. "No time for chitchat with the kids, ladies. You have some serious meeting and greeting to do." He stood as erect as he could, bent over his walker.

Dash's heart leaped in her throat; trading introductions with a hundred strangers did not count as one of her favorite things. But Ben seemed to understand. He swept her, not into a cluster of strangers, but rather into group clustered about someone she knew. "Randa! So good to see you."

Randa Saunders, who had made her billions supplying pipeline infrastructure for nations great and small, glowed with joy at seeing her. "Dash!" She looked Dash up and down, and drawled, "I hardly recognize you without your lab coat."

Dash laughed and spun lightly. "*Bu* Amanda insisted I hang it up for today."

One of the strangers in the group spoke up. "It's a beautiful dress." He introduced himself.

This began a round of introductions to people she did not know but whom all seemed to know her. Randa regaled everyone with stories about how Dash had rejuvenated her. Dash felt her face burning.

A male voice interrupted, "Randa, I'm afraid I have to steal your heroine."

Dash turned, chin up and eyes alight. "Colin!" She nodded to Randa and her troupe and did not quite scamper to Colin's side. "Thank you for the rescue."

Colin's eyes twinkled. "Rescue? You may have to hold off on your thanks. I'd like you to meet Toni."

Dash sighed. "My throat is quite dry. Could I get a Coke first?"

Colin bowed. "As you wish. But then it's back into the torture chamber."

The man standing alertly before the Chief Advisor's Resolute desk wore a white silk shirt, black tie, and a black suit. With his short haircut and ramrod-straight back, a casual observer might have guessed he was a retired soldier.

In reality, Darren was nothing of the sort. The Army had thrown him aside after the psych evaluation had scientifically categorized him with acute antisocial personality disorder. To be more precise, he was a sadistic whack job. Darren led the tiny team that reported directly to the Chief Advisor, responsible for the branch of governmental intelligence collection euphemistically referred to as "strict interrogation." The Chief Advisor tasted bile in his throat as he thought about how strict Darren's interrogations tended to be.

It was all perfectly legal. After an incident in which two

tourists from Illinois had been blown up while visiting the Smithsonian in Washington, all the Red state congressmen had stood shoulder-to-shoulder with half the Blue state congressmen to vote for the new powers granted the new team. News media from BreitTart to Huffington heralded it as a remarkable demonstration of bipartisanship.

As Darren reported on his investigations, he lit up with excitement. The Chief Advisor had gotten used to this. Whether the news was good or bad, Darren always lit up as he thought about the techniques he had used to obtain the information.

Alas, the Chief Advisor already knew from Darren's sober posture that the news on the latest interrogation would disappoint. Surprising. Darren never failed to get the answers he sought. Except, of course, on those occasions when the prisoner didn't actually *know* the answers.

The Chief Advisor decided to warm up the conversation with an easy question. "I take it the transfer of Kelly and Kurt went smoothly?" He already knew that it had gone fine, of course, since he'd been following the progress of these prisoners very closely. Not only did they hold critical information required for the survival of the State, but also the prisoners had cost so much. The concessions he'd had to make to the Canadian prime minister to get those kidnappers had been egregious. He frowned as he thought with irritation about the BrainTrust's refusal to send the kidnappers to him in the first place. It was, after all, in the BrainTrust's best interests as well as his own to find their employer.

Darren answered, "Yes, the transfer was straightforward." He smiled wickedly. "I don't think the prisoners were very happy with the outcome, however."

"Judging by your earlier lack of expression, I take it Kelly and Kurt have not yet been helpful in the search for their employer." What the Chief Advisor had known before prisoner delivery was that Kurt and Kelly had gone to the BrainTrust with the intention of kidnapping the doctor developing the Fountain of Youth. Fortunately, they had been foiled by some girl they claimed had been a commando from the Pakistani army. The Chief Advisor had scoffed at first—surely the Pakistanis would never let a woman into the Army, much less into the commandos— but his own people had assured him that such women existed. It seemed all too reasonable in retrospect to predict that one of them would find their way to that damnable cluster of sardine cans.

Darren was still speaking, reluctantly it seemed, to the Chief Advisor. "They continued to insist through our final interrogation that they'd been hired by the Premier of the Russian Union. Through intermediaries, of course."

The Advisor shook his head. "That's obviously ridiculous. The Premier's a personal friend of mine."

Darren grimaced. "Of course, sir. I know that, sir. Which is why, even though I'm now convinced Kelly thought he was telling the truth, we knew it was just a lie. That's why we continued to interrogate them to the end."

The Chief Advisor was puzzled. Darren was once again speaking as if he were done with the interrogation. Odd. "Well, I want you to continue to question them."

Darren's shoulders slumped. "I'm afraid that will not be

possible, sir. They did not survive the last round of questioning."

Ah. Mystery solved. "Oh, my."

Darren's embarrassment was palpable; he'd never lost a prisoner this way before. "I assure you it won't happen again. I was so certain they knew something that I...got a little carried away."

This was, of course, the risk of hiring people well-suited to the job. A necessary risk. The Advisor waved for him to continue.

"We hypothesize Kurt and Kelly were hired by someone with the ability to set up a false trail to the Premier. Everything about the false trail was, in fact, essentially perfect. My entire team investigated the diligent efforts Kelly made to track down his true employer. We all believe he should have been successful in uncovering the frame-up."

"Aha. So the employer is someone of exceptional wealth, power, and competence."

"Yes, sir. Someone with assets comparable to those of the Premier."

The Chief Advisor looked thoughtful. "Though of course, it couldn't actually be him."

Darren looked abjectly glum. He paused as some sort of desire wrenched his face, but in the end he meekly answered, "Of course, sir. That is," the pain on Darren's face grew more acute, as if *he* were being tortured, "exactly the conclusion we drew."

After Darren departed, the Chief Advisor found himself staring, unseeing, through the window into the Rose Garden. Who had that kind of power? Wheeler, of course.

But Wheeler wouldn't send someone to kidnap his own people.

Who else? The technologically sophisticated democracies had too much oversight. What about the Chinese President for Life? This would require some thought.

As Colin ordered a Coke for her, Dash found herself drawn to a painting on the wall done in an oriental style. Except, as she scrutinized it, it was not a painting, exactly. The caption told her this was the *Great Wave off Kanagawa*, but it had been done in a sort of pointillist style…with emeralds and sapphires to render the wave, and diamonds and opals representing the white foam.

Colin handed her a drink. "Ostentatious, is it not?"

Dash just shook her head. "Beautiful as well. Breathtaking, even." She took a fortifying sip of her Coke and Colin led her back into the crowd, scanning the faces.

Jam interrupted him. "Colin. Good to see you."

Colin looked down and smiled. "Jam. Ping. You both look utterly lovely. Why aren't you surrounded by a dozen young men?"

Jam looked away. "I think they may be intimidated."

Ping disagreed. "Not intimidated enough." She nudged Jam and flicked her eyes at two men watching them. "We may have to demonstrate our skills. I'll bet everyone would enjoy watching."

Dash frowned. "No beating up the guests. Not without good reason."

Colin smiled. "I'm glad I caught up with you two. Dash, you should hear this as well."

All three watched Colin expectantly.

"Ping, Jam, you've been promoted. Ping, you'll be the Security Chief for the Prometheus archipelago. Jam, you're the Expedition Commander for the Fuxing."

Everyone looked at him in astonishment. Ping spoke. "Are you crazy? What happens the next time someone comes for Dash?"

Colin waved the objection away. "Don't fret, I've got her covered. We're going to try a more subtle approach this time."

Ping scrunched her face. "What if we don't want to go?"

Dash touched Ping's arm lightly. "I'm sure I'll be ok. You two should go where you are most needed. Surely being the Security Chief for a whole archipelago is both important and a huge opportunity."

Colin added, "Particularly for an archipelago headed to Africa, with all those pirates."

Ping's eyes glowed. "Pirates. I've always wanted to fight pirates."

Jam interrupted this reverie. "What exactly is an 'Expedition Commander?'"

Colin explained, "You'll be going dirtside to seek out new life amidst old civilizations." His eyes glinted. "Specifically, you'll look for bright lives that need new opportunities, the people we need to join the Fuxing and make it a success. Lenora Thornhill will brief you in detail when you get there."

Jam considered this. "So, I'd be going into China? Wouldn't it make more sense to send Ping? She can at least speak the language, and blend in." She reflected on her words. "Ok, she couldn't *really* blend in, but she'd at least know the customs."

Ping answered, "Jam, suppose we were sending an expedition to Waziristan, your home. You'd know the language and customs. Would you go yourself, or send me?"

Jam's eyes bulged. "I guess I see your point. If anyone recognized me, I'd be in deep trouble." She focused her attention more sharply on Ping as she drew the inevitable conclusion. "Which means that if anyone recognized *you*—"

Colin interrupted. "Anyway, Lenora thinks Jam here is an excellent choice. The mission is more important than is immediately obvious."

Dash's eyes brimmed with tears. "I miss you both already." They all stood in quiet sorrow.

Ping broke the spell. "Group hug." She grabbed them both. The background music switched again, *"Ground Control to Major Tom..."*

Colin harrumphed. "I see Toni. Time to go."

Clutching the drink, Dash smiled as Colin made the intro.

Toni reached out to shake her hand as Colin continued, "This is Captain Shatzki of the Israeli Air Force. Toni, this is Dr. Dyah Ambarawati."

"Call me Dash."

Toni nodded, her eyes alight with amusement. "Dash it is, then."

Dash grinned as she looked levelly at Toni, who was her height. "At last, someone I can look at eye-to-eye." She glanced around the room. Though Colin had managed to vanish already, plenty of people towered over her. "I always feel like I am surrounded by trees here on the BrainTrust."

"I get that. Any time it frustrates me, I just rent a laser tag copter and go shoot some of them down." She shrugged. "I'm delighted to meet you. As you may already suspect, you're the talk of the party."

"I would have thought the SpaceR launch was the talk of the party."

Toni acknowledged this. "Well, that too." A mischievous gleam lit her face. "But you're now known, at least among the old guard in this crowd, as 'Dr. Dash who is *not* working on the Fountain of Youth.'" She cocked her head to the left. "You see Dawn Rainer holding court over there, right?"

Dash looked at the ring of enraptured listeners, most of whom were geriatric, listening as the new queen of the Rainer media empire talked. Dash heard the word "Anne," and had a sinking feeling that Dawn was waxing poetic about how Dash's therapy had cured Dawn's mother of dementia...for a couple of hours before the therapy killed her.

Meanwhile, Dash could see across the room that yet another group had gathered around Randa, all spellbound by whatever story she was telling. Randa stroked her face as she concluded, her eyes moist with tears, and her audience clapped softly in appreciation. Dash was quite certain she knew what story Randa was telling. Dash groaned. "We must tighten the confidentiality clause in the contracts with our patients," she muttered.

Toni laughed lightly, a warm and sympathetic sound of joy. "You're far too late for that." Toni nodded in another direction. This time Dash could see Lucas Kahn across the room, looking back at her, smiling softly, now waving at her since she'd noticed him. He turned away. "Kahn's friends will be more of a problem for you, you know. He actually *looks* younger. No one who knows him can help being astonished when they see him for the first time, after what you did for him."

Dash felt a desperate need to change the subject. "So you're a captain in the Israeli Air Force. What brings you to the BrainTrust?"

"Well, technically, I'm a reservist at the moment. I'm pursuing a degree in aerospace engineering at BTU."

"How delightful. Are you thinking of getting a job with SpaceR? Because Matt—the CEO—has become something of a friend of mine. I could introduce you."

Toni shook with laughter, setting her emerald solitaire pendant dancing. "Well, I'd be delighted to be introduced, but honestly, it'll be a while before I can look for a job. Commitments to my country and my father, you know."

Dash nodded. "Of course." She had an idea. "Perhaps I should introduce you to Ping, a friend of mine who I am sure would enjoy hearing stories of flying fighter planes."

Toni looked into the distance and touched her cheek, much the way Jam touched the scar on her cheek. "Fighting is not always fun, I'm afraid." And Dash knew she should first introduce Toni to Jam.

Another thought crossed Dash's mind, and she giggled.

"So, you know everybody here is *Somebody*, right? Are you really an Air Force captain, or do you have a secret identity? What is the nature of your...*Somebodiness?*"

Toni just shook her head. "I suspect I owe my presence to my father. He couldn't be here, but he is certainly *Somebody.*"

"So who—"

A brilliant flash of light interrupted the conversation, which turned out to be from a camera. Dash blinked several times before she could see that a third person had joined the conversation. "Dr. *'This can be improved upon'* Dash, I presume?" the new person said a little too loudly. "I'm Lindsey Postrel, editor of Cogent News. You know how they say the BrainTrust is 'The Last Stand of the Creative Human Spirit?'" Before Dash could even acknowledge the question, Lindsey took half a step closer and drove on. "Well, Cogent is the last news source of the thinking human mind." She raised her glass in a toast, perhaps to her publication. "Liberated, not Regulated."

She turned toward Dawn Rainer. Lindsey switched hands to hold up three fingers at Dawn. "Ha! Read between the lines, Dawn, you bitch." She cleared her throat and took another half step closer to Dash. "So, I hear you fixed her mother, however temporarily."

Dash demurred, "I hope to do better in the future."

Toni, who had been watching as Lindsey pushed into Dash's personal space, squeezed in front of Lindsey. "Back it up, bitch," she snarled.

Dash was shocked, but Lindsey took a step back, laughing. "So the Doc has yet another protector, I see. Captain Shatzki, nice to meet you too." Lindsey's whole posture relaxed as she slid her weight sideways onto her left hip. "Stay cool. Fact is, I'm one of the Doc's protectors too. As is the entire Rainer clan, for that matter." She surveyed the room, nodding periodically as she assessed faces. "Actually, her protectors may outnumber everyone else in the party."

Toni still had her hands balled into fists. "Who do you think you can protect her from?"

Lindsey blinked in surprise. "Are you kidding? Breit-Tart, and all the fake news generators of their ilk."

Dash gave her a puzzled expression. "Why would I care what they say about me? Why would they say anything at all about me anyway?"

Lindsey stared at her open-mouthed and speechless.

Before Lindsey could articulate an answer, Ben wheeled his walker up to them. "Lindsey, delighted you could make it." He looked at Toni's expression and guessed the reason. "Dash, sorry Lindsey's harassing you."

Lindsey put a hand on her hip and pouted, and Ben laughed. "Since you're here and Dash is here, I think it's photo time."

Lindsey rolled her eyes. "As you wish." She looked at Dash. "In addition to doing serious journalism with Cogent, I write the occasional puff piece for Ben here. Actual news is currently out of style, so it's hard to make a living with it. But I feel confident that'll change. Reality has a way of making itself felt in the long run," she finished dryly.

Ben proceeded to have Toni drag people over for photos in no order Dash understood. Matt and *Pak* Colin and *Bu* Amanda were among the first, but others followed. Soon Dawn sent her photographer to join Lindsey and came herself, then Randa and Lucas, and eventually strangers were snapping pics of each other with Dash and Ping and Jam and telling her how interested they were in her research, though they didn't seem at all interested in her explanations of it. She accepted seven digital business cards from people interested in becoming test subjects, eleven cards from people interested in investing, and four cards from people who wanted both, plus a card from the son of the man who had invented the kickswitch used in most apps. The son insisted on swapping contact info because he wanted to take her to dinner some time.

Ping urged her to take him up on the offer. "Find a restaurant you couldn't possibly afford, and let him pay for it," she suggested, laughing.

Dash's head swirled. She had thought she was reasonably good with names, but the crowd threatened to swamp her mind.

At one point Lindsey sidled up to her and said, as if reading her mind, "Don't worry about it. Ben keeps a photo catalog of everyone who attends these things. You can look up anyone you need after the party." Lindsey whirled away before Dash could thank her.

Dash suspected she looked like a deer in headlights when an enormous bear of a man with thick eyebrows stepped up beside her. An oversized diamond adorned his tie clasp, and a matching one adorned the ring on his finger. "Dr. Dash! I know, I know, I should just call you Dash. Allow me to pretend that you and I are old friends so I can impress the crowd. My name is Dmitri Mikhailov."

He nodded toward the door from Ben's cabin—Dash

realized *Bu* Amanda had been right, this wasn't a cabin, it was a mansion—out to the hallway.

Dmitri continued, "I'm Ben's neighbor just across the hallway. If you'd like to escape from this madness, would you care to take a stroll, see my place? I assure you it is much quieter. And much nicer than Ben's little place here, of course."

Dash hesitated, wondering if she should let her friends know she was leaving. But Jam was on the second-floor balcony in deep conversation with Lucas Kahn's youngest son. Judging by the handwaving, they were comparing Jam's time parachute jumping in the commandos with David's time skydiving. Dash thought that would be an interesting comparison. She knew Jam hated jumping from airplanes, while David, according to Lucas, loved soaring over the BrainTrust.

Meanwhile, Ping was leaning back against the grand piano, one foot propped up on the bench. She held her long diamond necklace in the middle and spun the bottom half in circles while regaling three young men with tall tales. Tales, judging by the way she twisted her body, of her time pretending to be a hooker.

Dash couldn't think of a single reason to interrupt them. She turned to Dmitri and nodded to the door. "I would be delighted to find someplace a little quieter for a little while."

The noise level dropped dramatically as they entered the

hallway, and faded to a hushed silence as they entered Dmitri's lair.

Dmitri exhaled heavily. "Much better. I can hear myself think again."

Dash agreed, "Me, too." She paused as two hulking men appeared and bowed to her, and two others hung back.

Dmitri explained, "Pay no attention to my assistants here." He started pointing, "Alexei and Vasily here, and Gleb and Yefim in the back."

Alexei continued to stare at Dash with an intensity that made her uncomfortable.

Dmitri glared at him as he spoke to Dash. "Let me refresh your drink here and show you around." He leaned over and whispered something in Russia to Alexei. Dash didn't know the language, but the tone sounded for all the world like a man telling his attack dog to "Stay."

The main salon was, Dash had to admit, quite sumptuous. As Dmitri refilled her glass of Coke, a work of art close to the balcony windows caught her attention. The caption stated that it was a view of Mt. Vesuvius from Portici, but it was not a painting. Like the Great Wave in Ben's dwelling, it was a pointillist rendition done in rare gems. Whereas Ben's wave had water rendered in emeralds and sapphires, here the flames of the eruption were done in rubies and a yellow gem she did not recognize.

Dmitri handed her the drink. "Beautiful, isn't it?" He pointed at the gems she didn't know. "Yellow imperial topaz, once reserved exclusively for the Russian tsars. Quite rare."

"It's beautiful." One other thing Dash noticed was that this picture was twice as large as the one in Ben's place.

Dash began to sense a theme, which Dmitri confirmed with his next words.

"Ben Wilson's pad is four thousand square feet. Mine is five thousand," he noted with grand pride.

Dash didn't know what to say, so she moved to look out the window. Dmitri opened the sliding doors onto the balcony. "Let's get a little fresh air in here."

Dash stepped out into the crisp air. "So, Dmitri, what do you do for a living? Or is that not a proper question at a party like this?"

Dmitri waved his hand majestically at the sea. "What party? The party's back there. Here there are just the two of us. Ask anything." He took a sip of his drink; some form of scotch or bourbon, Dash guessed. "I'm an industrialist, like half the people on the *Haven*. I specialize in munitions." He guffawed. "You know, a baby-killer. At least that's what the American press says about me."

Dash felt a little sick. "And… are you?"

Dmitri shrugged. "I'm either the baby-killer or the baby-defender, depending on who I sell my munitions to. When I'm selling to my personal customers, I tend to be a baby-defender." His voice took on a darker tone. "But when I'm doing deals on behalf of the Premier, it's not so good." With a note of barely-controlled rage, he growled, "When I'm working for the Premier, I'm pretty much a murderer."

Dash stared at him making such a candid admission. "Why don't you stop? It looks like you have enough money to do whatever you want."

Dmitri laughed. "It's not that simple. But there's good news; it won't be complicated for much longer. The

Premier's not a young man." The knuckles on his hand turned white as he clenched his glass. "I can outlive him."

He shook himself. "Aren't you cold out here? Such a little thing as you, wearing a dress like that? Which I'd mention is beautiful, by the way, except I'm sure everyone else has said that already, and I so hate following the crowd." He gestured back into the mansion. "Come, let me show you the rest of my place." He turned to lead the way, then, as if suddenly remembering something, added, "And my yacht! Today's not the day for it, but you simply must let me take you out for a cruise some time. My *Buccaneer's* the biggest mega-yacht here."

"Of that I am sure," Dash agreed, without necessarily agreeing to go for a cruise.

Alexei stood near the entrance, watching Dmitri show off his absurd collection of garish art and ridiculous trappings. He spoke softly. "I still say we should just take her, here and now. The party's full of noise and crazy rich people, so no one will notice she's missing until we're long gone."

Vasily shushed him. "Don't look now, but Ping and Jam just slid into the passage from Ben's place. If you think they won't notice, you've got a screw loose."

Alexei shrugged. "So we invite them in and take them too. We're Spetsnaz, for heaven's sake." He turned slowly, pretending to just become aware of the ladies for the first time, and smiled.

Vasily groaned. "Rapists and mass murderers smile the same way you do. Stop it."

Turning away, Alexei continued his assessment. "Surely we can take a Pakistani girl and an itty-bitty ninja."

Vasily closed his eyes for a moment. "Of course we can, but there's a considerable risk someone would hear us. And if the noise or the bodies reached the passageway, the security vidcams would light up like Christmas trees."

Alexei grunted.

Ping nodded to Alexei as he smiled at them. She whispered to Jam, "He looks just like a rapist or mass murderer when he smiles, don't you think?"

Jam put her hand on Ping's shoulder. "Relax. He's just being a bodyguard."

"Yeah, but he doesn't have to be so obvious about it." Ping grinned at Jam. "He'd look a lot less conspicuous if he wore a Karl Lagerfeld ensemble the way Dash's bodyguard does."

Jam laughed softly. "I think he'd look very conspicuous in Chanel."

Ping twirled her diamond necklace. "I just can't help thinking there's something wrong here. Maybe it's just the rumor Colin told us that the Russian Union Premier was behind that kidnapping attempt. Or maybe I just have a strange imagination—"

"You're just bored and want some action."

"But I can't help wishing I had my *chura*—your *chura*—with me."

Jam refrained from pointing out there was no place Ping could conceal a *chura* in her current dress. Well, one place, but Jam refused to think about that. "If it comes to that, you can probably use your Vivienne as a garrote."

Ping brightened. "You think?" She stopped twirling the necklace, and held it in both hands thoughtfully, snapping it taut several times as she looked at Alexei. "You don't think it would break, would it?"

From the corner of his eye, Vasily caught the sudden halt of the spinning necklace. Studying Ping's face, he muttered to Alexei, "And now the itty bitty ninja looks like she's measuring your neck for a garrote."

Alexei rolled his eyes. "Honestly, you have the strangest imagination."

Eventually, Dmitri escorted Dash back to the door, from whence Jam and Ping escorted her back to the main party. Gleb and Yefim drifted up.

Gleb observed admiringly to Dmitri, "I have to say, boss, you were really convincing as you explained to Dash how much you hated the Premier. If she were at all suspicious you work for him before, she certainly isn't now. I believed you hated him myself."

Dmitri growled but continued to smile in case Dash and company looked back. "No acting required, Gleb. That murdering scumbag may have given me the monopoly I needed to become a billionaire, but he's given me plenty of reasons to hate him. Plenty and more."

Alexei couldn't let the opportunity to complain again pass. "I *still* say we could have taken her right here, right now, Ping and Jam included."

Dmitri laughed gruffly, slapping Alexei on the shoulder. "But it would be so much easier without Ping and Jam, wouldn't it? And I just overheard good news. Colin is sending those two away when the Fuxing and Prometheus fleets depart."

Gleb, Yefim, and Vasily visibly relaxed, and Gleb spoke for them all. "Thank heaven. Without those two hanging around, this'll be smoother than we ever dreamed."

Alexei grumbled, "But it won't be half as much fun."

A grim aura hung over the governor's office. The news media were all howling. Blue media howled with rage that SpaceR, their beloved rocket company, had betrayed them by stealing the state's money and offshoring their launches. The fact that a majority of SpaceR rockets still launched from Texas for equatorial orbits was overlooked. SpaceR was a California company, so it needed to launch rockets from California.

The Red media simply howled in laughter at the way the California government had once again bitten off its own nose to spite its own face.

The governor kept resetting his worried expression to a poker face. The new plan for punishing SpaceR was his idea, as simple as it was effective. But somehow every time the BrainTrust got involved, even the simplest plans got complicated.

The Attorney General was once again riding high on his elation at the new plan. "I can see why you're the governor. This is a brilliant solution to the problem. We're going to make those bastards scream for mercy. With punitive damages, we'll be able to balance the budget for years." He sagged sideways a little. "Well, maybe not that long. With the new funding stream straight from SpaceR revenues, there are a lot of new government programs we could start." He straightened up again. "We should announce it today. That'll put a damper on their celebration." In the governor's office, they had the wallscreen tied to live coverage of the impending launch. They would watch it firsthand, along with just about everybody else in the world.

The governor shook his head. "We are not going to announce it today, or tomorrow. Our message would just get swallowed up in the wave of SpaceR news media coverage. No, we'll let them have a couple of days of cheering, then we'll knock them cold in the next news cycle."

The Attorney General acquiesced. "You're the boss. And besides, you're probably right. Wait till they're standing tall before we knock 'em down." He frowned for a moment, then a big grin erupted across his face. "Besides, the rocket could blow up on the pad, and wipe out the BrainTrust with it."

The governor brightened considerably. "Good point. I had forgotten that possibility."

Matt Toscano, like the governor, found himself reflecting

on the possibility of an explosion, though his reaction to these thoughts was quite different. "At least get everyone indoors if you're not going to move the fleet farther away. You can make them all move indoors, can't you?"

Colin replied in soothing tones, "Relax. We closed all the gangways. Everyone is going to be inside for the duration. We made special arrangements so everyone should be able to get window seats to watch the show."

Matt breathed a sigh of relief. "Great. What about evacuations? Did a lot of people take you up on the opportunity to take a ferry ride and get away from here?"

Colin chuckled. "And miss the biggest party of the decade? Are you kidding? Understand that the BrainTrust population is heavily tilted toward young people eager to see the future become better. You know the ferries we commissioned to take people away?" He paused for a dramatic moment. "Those ships arrived full of friends and family of the BrainTrusters, all of whom wanted to come aboard to watch the launch. The ferries left empty."

Matt just lowered his face into his hands.

Colin slapped him on the back. "Cheer up. If this goes as badly as you fear, you and I will not be around to take the blame."

At that moment a beautiful soprano voice, trained to project by a decade of leading cheers, sang through the crowd. "Matt!" his wife called. Gina waved at them from across the room so vigorously it set her hair swaying. Her hair, a brilliant fire-red with streaks of blonde running through, was said by her most viciously polite enemies to be her finest feature, and did great credit to her hair stylist. Gina herself claimed her hair was naturally that way, mostly correctly. She sashayed up to them wearing a navy strapless mermaid dress with gold embellishments.

Matt hugged her fiercely and put his mouth to her ear. "You have to leave now," he ordered. "I'll arrange a yacht to take you farther away, where you'll be safer."

She kissed him on the cheek. "I love you too, darling."

And the ship-wide speaker system, tied for the moment into a BrainTrust's net, started droning out the final countdown.

Thousands of rocket launches like this one had occurred over the course of the preceding decades. A certain mundane dreariness should have cast a gray pall over the events over time. There were YouTube videos beyond count of such launches.

But for human beings with their hardwired fascination with fire and its kindred phenomena, the thrill never faded. People would have held their breaths as they watched just another launch from Vandenberg or Boca Chica. For this launch, in this place, they held their heartbeats.

The lambent flame billowed from beneath the rockets. Those on the upper decks could now see the purpose of the black lines that emerged from the pad and extended to both the port and starboard sides. They were flame trenches, down which the fury of the exhaust gases flooded in brilliant burning light that submerged the impervious black tiles.

Up the ship went, oh so slowly. Surely, *surely*, such a tall narrow structure must topple over, destroying itself, the ship, and most of the people watching.

Instead, it continued to rise. Eventually, it tilted as it sought orbit.

On the *Haven*, attention turned to a series of large display screens hooked to cameras holding steady on the ship through a telescopic lens. There was an explosion, sudden, terrible. More than one person screamed in horror.

Matt laughed explosively. "Nothing to worry about, folks," he asserted in strong, commanding tones. "That's just the first stage separating. Everything is good." He took a pair of short breaths. Quietly, he said in disbelief, "Everything is good." He wiped a hand across his eyes. He did not have tears in them. Absolutely not.

Gina hugged him. "Congratulations, lover boy."

Ben raised his champagne glass high and shouted, "Congratulations to SpaceR and the BrainTrust!"

A chorus of congratulations roared in his wake.

Applause erupted throughout Ben's abode. People stepped back, leaving Matt and Gina in the middle of an empty space. Gina nudged him. "Say something, dearest."

This was not Matt's thing, but he would make do. "To the future!" he roared. Then, considering the audience, "To the BrainTrust!"

Many of the older billionaires toasted only half-heartedly, but the young ones understood and answered in kind.

And then it was over. Matt put down his glass. As Ben came up to him, Matt said, "We have to go. They'll be waiting for me on the *Argus*."

"All of SpaceR and half of everyone else, I imagine," Ben said dryly. "You better hurry."

Matt crooked his elbow, and Gina put her arm through his. Matt searched the crowd, spotted someone he needed, and pointed. "Dash, come with me." Gina nudged him again, forcefully this time. "Please," he added.

Dash looked at him in surprise. Then Jam had her by one arm, Ping by the other, pushing her forward. "Go," they said in unison. Ping continued, "Celebrate with the people who actually made it happen."

Matt grabbed Colin as well on the way out.

At the elevator to take them up to the copter pad, Colin begged off. "I'll catch up with you on the *Argus* in a few minutes." And he was off.

When they reached the copter pad, Gina released her grip on her husband and grabbed Dash. "You're with me." She guided Dash to a beautiful navy-blue copter.

"I've gotta rush," Matt said. He turned to the thin teenager standing next to his machine. "Let's go, Ted."

Ted, who looked too young to drive a car much less a helicopter, hopped into the pilot's seat and brought the copter blades up to speed while Colin slid into the passenger seat. Like almost all the homebrew copters on the BrainTrust, Ted's machine could carry only two passengers.

Gina yelled, "You're in a hurry, huh? You can't possibly beat us with that old slug."

Ted's yell of disagreement was drowned by the whirring of the copter blades.

Gina slid into the pilot's seat after coaxing Dash in on the passenger side.

Matt and Ted got off the pad first, and Ted cranked her up to full speed. They were well on their way when the navy-blue copter flew up next to them. Gina waved gaily and egged Dash into waving as well, then buzzed past.

In his head, Matt could hear his wife laughing wickedly at him. He grumbled, "Can't we go any faster?"

Ted watched them sail into the distance admiringly. "She looks like one sweet ride, Mr. Toscano."

Matt was about to clock his pilot when he realized Ted was referring to the machine, not the woman.

Ted continued, oblivious, "We can't go any faster with this copter. She's right, you know. This one is obsolete." He paused, licked his lips, "You know, this was the first copter I ever designed. I could build a much better one now. Really fast."

A glint rose in Matt's eyes. "Fast enough to leave her in the dust?"

"Absolutely, Mr. Toscano."

Matt touched Ted lightly on the shoulder. "Congratulations, Ted. You just got yourself an angel investor."

On Minerva Avenue, a fluke of atmospheric conditions allowed the sound of the SpaceR rocket to reach a little girl. She ran into the living room, grabbed her kitten, and tugged on her mother. Once her mother stood up, she grabbed her father and dragged them both out under the invulnerable roof that would protect them all from the rocket. They huddled together, the little girl shivering in the middle.

After the sound had passed, she handed her kitty to her mother and reached out with both arms to hug her parents. "Mom, Dad, I love you so much."

4

ENDINGS AND BEGINNINGS

Merit tokens can be exchanged for free time, sporting goods, and lab equipment for your own independent research.
 —Accel Educational Framework. Topic: Introduction. Module: Student Rewards.

The departures of the BrainTrust Fuxing and the Brain-Trust Prometheus fleets had been postponed till the successful First Launch. Two days had passed since then, and now it was time for everyone to go. Ping, Jam, and Dash stood on the *Argus* at the gangway that would take Jam and Ping to the *Mount Parnassus* of the Prometheus fleet. More interconnecting gangways would take them through the *Mount Helicon* of the Fuxing fleet, thence on to the *Taixue* where everyone from the fleets was gathering for final briefings.

Ping was eager to roll. Since the Prometheus fleet was being dispatched to Africa, she was certain she'd have the chance to fight pirates. Since Colin had told her she was going, she'd been practicing with her Big Gun continuously. "Don't shoot till you see the whites of their eyes," Ping said excitedly, tapping the weapon strapped to her back. "Of course, with the digital sights on this baby, you can see the whites of their eyes from fifty kilometers."

Jam was unimpressed. "Only if you can hold it steady enough to see at that resolution without jumping kilometers every which way before you can blink. And your Big Gun is bigger than you are, Ping." Jam thought back over the past forty-eight hours, which had been a whirlwind.

The day after Colin had promoted Jam to Expedition Commander for the Fuxing, she'd confronted him and Amanda and argued against it. Jam had patiently explained that she was not qualified to run a team. They had patiently explained to her that no one is *ever* qualified to run a team, and all too often the ones who think they are, are in fact the least qualified.

Next Jam had demanded, "Which peacekeepers are you putting into our cabin next to hers?"

Colin had shaken his head. "No peacekeepers, Jam. As I said earlier, we're going with a more subtle approach during the next phase of her research. Trust me." He paused, watching her eyes. "You *do* trust me, don't you? It all worked out OK last time, right?"

Amanda had joined Jam in just staring at him suspiciously.

In the end, he had just laughed. "Go, take the next step. You'll be back with Dash soon enough I promise."

Jam had just rolled her eyes. "Very well, Colin Wheeler. We are counting on you."

Now the last members of both new BrainTrust fleets were boarding. Dash, Jam, and Ping were still huddled together by the gangway. Everyone was holding back tears.

Ping shouted, "Group hug!" And they did.

Jam whispered in Dash's ear, "Take care, girlfriend."

Dash answered them, "You are the ones sailing into danger. Be careful."

Ping said brightly, "Cheer up! If we're lucky, you'll need to come out to the Prometheus to patch me up after I wipe out all the pirates."

With that, Ping and Jam walked down the gangway, waved goodbye one last time, and disappeared.

Dash stood quietly for a long moment. Colin appeared. "They will come back, you know. Stronger and better. Who knows? Perhaps even wiser."

Dash watched as the tunnel-bridge connecting the gangways retracted into the side of the ship. "The places they are going are dangerous," she observed.

"Which is exactly why we're sending Jam and Ping. Who better to handle it?"

Eventually, Dash forced herself to answer. As was her nature, she answered honestly. "True."

An alarm went off on Colin's tablet. "Gotta go."

He walked off. Dash watched as the isle ship broke away and headed into the west, for a very long time.

In the early days of Mao's revolutionary transformation of China, the power structure was quite simple: the chairman's closest personal friends held all the power. With Mao's death, the process of achieving authority became considerably more Darwinian. Power passed to the most ruthless, cunning, competent, and hungry members of the elite.

But as time passed, the winners of this ferocious process of natural selection had discovered they had a problem. Their children were not getting any smarter, and they were not getting any younger. So the system evolved once more, in the way that such systems always evolve, and the instruments of state power were reshaped to protect the bloodlines of the power elite. Thus, early in the twenty-first century, a new class of characters came into being with their own name. The Red Princelings sprang forth, born to accept the power commanded by their parents when their time came.

By the time the ships of the Fuxing and Prometheus fleets departed from the BrainTrust, the transformation was complete. All power was hereditary. However, the qualities of ruthlessness, cunning, hunger, and competence had been transmitted from father to son to grandson as imperfectly as always. The ruthlessness had evolved an edge of cruelty, but still crossed generations with considerable success. The hunger utterly disappeared, and the cunning and competence suffered considerable impairment.

Occasional bright spots arose. Here and there, a grandchild would demonstrate a spike in disciplined intelligence, but more often all but the cruelty was lost.

Guang Jian sat looking out the window of the dean's office. Others might have found little in the view to hold their interest, since all he could see was thick gray fog, like a painter's canvas that had been exposed to too much car exhaust. On another day with a brighter sky, another person might have found some charm in the view of the greenswards of the university and the quaint stone architecture of the old town of Cambridge, England, but Guang Jian found the town no more exciting than the dull fog. Something even duller than the fog, however, filled the room: the droning voice of the dean.

"If you were anyone else, we would be putting you on trial. But…" The gray-haired fuddy-duddy pursed his lips as he clenched his pen. He sat behind an ancient desk surrounded by bookcases filled with ancient writings that made the room smell moldy, at least to Guang. "The guards will accompany you to your limo, which will take you to your father's airplane, which will take you home."

Guang Jian exhaled a sigh of relief as the droning stopped. He stood up. "I'll go pack my things."

The dean clenched his pen tighter. "No need. Your girlfriend, Fan Hui, has already put your things into the trunk of the car." The dean sighed. "We'll be sorry to lose her. It's a shame she's chosen to leave with you. She had a bright future here."

Guang Jian left without responding. Of course, Liu Fan Hui was leaving with him. He was the son of a member of the Standing Committee. Fan's father, while powerful enough in his own right, was merely a member of the

Politburo. Had she not wanted to leave with him, he would have demanded it, and she would have left with him anyway.

As their private jet arched away from the cold, miserable little island of Britain, Guang asked Fan, "How long until we land in Beijing, anyway?" He asked with a certain amount of dread. When his father droned at him the same way the dean had, he would have to listen.

Fan shook her head, and her long, glossy black hair reflected glints of light. It was one of the things he loved about her, the way her hair shimmied down her long, lithe back to almost touch her cute butt when she walked. "We aren't going to Beijing. We're going to Shanghai, where we'll board Chen Ying's mom's yacht and sail out to the new BrainTrust." Seeing Guang's blank look that perfectly blended ignorance with disinterest, Fan uttered a disgusted sound. "Honestly, you need to pay a little attention to what's happening in the world. The BrainTrust has sent a new archipelago to set up shop in international waters just outside our two hundred-mile territorial limit. It's called 'the *Fuxing*.' You know, the ancient God of Prosperity."

Now boredom congealed on Guang's features. "What could they possibly have that would be interesting?"

"They have a brand-new university, a branch of BTU. So they're already pretty prestigious, even though they don't have any students yet. They're calling it Taixue University."

For the first time, Guang showed a little interest. "So we'll have the run of the place?"

Fan nodded. "Exactly. We can mold it and run it as we

see fit." She frowned. "At least, we can run it if you learn to keep your pants zipped."

Dash took an arvee, one of the little driverless vehicles used on the BrainTrust to get around that looked more like a Disney bumper car than anything else, back to her cabin on the Appalachian Spring floor of the *Chiron*. There she found a tall, lean young woman with shoulder-length black hair, dusky skin, and a solid sleeve of tattoo-work running down her right arm. The tattooed beauty busily carried suitcases into the cabin next to hers—Ping and Jam's cabin, as Dash had always thought of it. Dash gripped her irritation and pushed it down. This woman had not caused her friends' departure.

The arvee stopped, Dash stepped out, and the new neighbor straightened from her labors. "Dr. Dash? Nice to meet you." She held out her hand in greeting.

Dash once more reflected on how irritatingly tall Americans were. She had to crane her neck to smile up at her. "Nice to meet you too. Just call me Dash. I guess you are my new neighbor."

"The pleasure is mine. My name is Chance. And I'm not just your new neighbor, I'm your new intern."

Dash paused for a moment. "Goodness. In that case, I am doubly-delighted to meet you. We are way behind schedule since…things did not work out with my last intern."

A shadow of concern crossed Chance's eyes. "I heard

what happened." She offered a sober smile. "I promise to be a better intern than he was."

Dash thought it best not to mention that prior to Byron's crazed attempt to kill her he had been a brilliant assistant, clearly capable of becoming a lead researcher in a few years in his own right. Chance would have to do well indeed to match him.

An arvan rolled up, and a bot hopped out and dropped two suitcases and a footlocker.

Chance nodded at the new packages, saying, "I guess my roommate is on her way."

Dash asked, "Do you know her?"

Chance shook her head. "They just assigned her last night. Her name is Toni."

"Toni?! Are you sure?" Dash asked.

And then another arvee rolled silently up.

Toni Shatski waved and leaped from the vehicle. "Dash! Great to see you again." She came over briskly and gave Dash an enthusiastic embrace, then turned. "And you must be Chance, my roommate, right?" More gingerly, Toni hugged her new roommate.

Dash was still staring at her. "I thought you were a student on the BTU ship. Should you not have a cabin over there?"

Toni shrugged. "I *am* a BTU student. But I guess Colin saw how well you and I got on together, so he asked if I'd mind having my home a little farther away." She paused. "As he pointed out, I'm a little older than the typical BTU kids. He thought I might like to hang out with people a little older, who didn't feel it necessary to pull all-nighters every time they had an exam."

Dash wondered if Toni would be disturbed when she found out how often Dash herself pulled all-nighters.

But Toni was still speaking. "Besides, it's only a kilometer and a bit, and I like to run 10K races. BTU is about four minutes away if I kick it a little."

Chance spoke. "That's cool. I'm a runner too." Her eyes lit up. "I hear there are some good paths around the archipelago." She turned to Dash. "I don't suppose you're a runner as well?"

Dash shook her head. "No. My knee..." Dash suddenly realized that her old reason for not running was now obsolete. She was still adjusting. "I used to have a bad knee. No cartilage." She brightened. "But they fixed that while I was in the hospital." For the bullet wound, she thought, but decided not to mention that. "I should be able to run now. Perhaps, if you don't mind a beginner ..."

Chance pumped her fist. "We're going to have so much fun."

Toni eyed Dash. "A newbie. We're going to have to break her in gently."

Chance's eyes lit up. "The beach. We'll start her off on the beach. The sand makes running really hard, but it soaks up the impact."

Toni agreed. "And we can wear bikinis. You'd get to show off all your tattoos."

Chance held up her arm to show off the line of tats. "And Dash would look great in a bikini." She clucked her tongue. "Wouldn't go very well with her lab coat, though."

While her two new neighbors rattled on discussing ever more ridiculous plans, Dash found herself studying them and thinking about their arrival on her doorstep. She was pretty sure Colin had put them both here deliberately, just like Ping and Jam.

Lindsey had already accused Toni of being one of her protectors. Could that mean... "Toni," Dash interrupted the comical discussion of how to be nearly naked on the beach without violating BrainTrust cultural conventions, "You're in the Air Force, correct? Do they teach you any hand-to-hand martial arts combat?"

Toni shrugged. "They taught me some Krav Maga. Honestly, I don't like it. I'm better with the parts of the style that're taken from aikido."

Dash persisted, "So, are you one of the top three Krav Maga experts or anything like that?"

Toni just laughed. "Oh, heavens no. Why?"

Dash turned to Chance. "And you. Are you a world champion martial arts expert in your spare time?"

Chance raised her eyebrows. "Well, I appeared in a few videos of mixed martial arts contests. They just loved my tattoos." She struck a pose. "I used to be a tattoo model."

Toni asked, "Not anymore? What happened?"

Chance sighed. "Started to run out of skin. Bioorganic here." She pointed at her arm again, where the web of tattoo work formed a complex pattern of conjoining curves. She then pulled the side of her skirt up and ran a finger down her left leg. "Biomechanical here." These tattoos also formed a pattern, but they consisted of sharp lines and hard angles. Chance turned and started lifting the back of her shirt. "And this is my best work—"

"OK, enough!" Dash laughed. "Save some for the beach."

Chance shrugged her shirt down again. "Anyway, I

decided it was time for a change of profession, so I got a scholarship here and came to work with you."

———

Ping and Jam had barely crossed the gangway onto the Mount Parnassus, an isle ship of the Fuxing archipelago, when a gruff older man wearing a captain's uniform accosted them. "And how are my two ferocious combat machines doing today?"

Jam's eyes gleamed in recognition. "Captain Ainsworth!" She saw someone else behind him. "And Chief Hart!" Her eyes danced. "Or should I call you 'Bruno?'"

Security Chief Hart Baddeley scowled at the nickname. "He calls me that when he wants me to pretend to have fifty pounds more and ten IQ points less." His scowl turned to a happy smile. "Call me Hart."

Jam stood awkwardly as the captain and the security chief came up and hugged her.

Ping smacked her lightly on the shoulder. "You're supposed to hug them back. After all, I guess they saved your life when they didn't throw you overboard, the way Drudge and Huffington say they're supposed to when they find stowaways." Ping stepped up and hugged them along with Jam.

Captain Jack Ainsworth finally pulled back, keeping a hand on Jam's shoulder as he examined her. Then he peered at Ping. "I hear the two of you have been busy, getting shot, being heroes, and so on and so forth." He chuckled. "About what I expected."

Ping offered a correction. "Jam was busy getting shot. I was busy being the hero."

Jam nodded. "All too true."

Hart guffawed. "Yeah, I'm sure that's the whole truth."

Ping hit him in the shoulder, glaring. "Just you remember it." She looked at both of them. "What're you doing here, anyway?"

Jack stood just the slightest bit straighter and tapped his spiffy new shoulder insignia. "After not throwing Jam overboard, they promoted us. I'm fleet captain for the Fuxing fleet. " He barked as if giving orders. "Listen up! You both report to me now!"

Ping stood up on her toes to confront him, bringing her head almost up to his chin. "Not me! I'm with the Brain-Trust Prometheus fleet."

Jack relaxed with a laugh. "Stand down, peacekeeper. Actually, Ping, you do report to me, if only temporarily."

Ping continued to glare at him, though she at least came down off her toes. "What are you talking about?"

Jam explained. "I tried to tell you this earlier, but you weren't listening. For the moment, our fleets have merged. Colin stole our manufacturing ship for SpaceR, and it's really not practical to run an archipelago without one. So you'll hook up with us off the coast of China while your manufacturing ship manufactures a new manufacturing ship for us."

Ping considered this for a moment, then lit up. "Cool! We're still together for a while."

Jack pretended to wipe sweat from his brow. "Glad you approve. Now, let me introduce you to the real people in charge."

Jam shook her head in puzzlement. "I thought you said you were the fleet captain. Don't you report directly to the BrainTrust consortium?"

Jack pointed the way to the elevators, Security Chief Hart bade his leave, and Jack led them onto the elevators and selected the destination. "Lothlorien deck," he ordered the elevator. "I do report to the BrainTrust. But the lines of command are not always hierarchically simple, as you two ought to know by now. I also report, under normal circumstances, to the Mission Commander. Or rather, the Mission Commanders, since we have two of them on board until we actually separate."

Jam immediately saw the problem. "Two Mission Commanders? And how do they resolve disputes when they disagree?"

The captain chortled. "Oh, they've been figuring out how to resolve disputes between the two of them for decades. If those two fight, just stand back and let them duke it out. They always deliver a good show."

The elevator doors opened, and they stepped out into a passage where the walls were decorated so that brilliant sunlight seemed to filter through the leaves of immense trees. Spiral staircases circled the stout trunks to treehouses barely visible from the ground. They walked across a patch of decking made to look like a bridge of living wood, with a deep blue roaring stream beneath them. They turned through an entrance into a hut.

Except that behind the entrance, instead of a hut, they found a large well-equipped lab with many tables. Not a research lab, but rather a teaching lab where students would gather to perform chemistry experiments, or in this case, biology experiments. Despite the high-power ventilation system found on all isle ships, a whiff of formaldehyde hung in the air.

A young woman with ivory skin and sea-green hair that matched her sea-green eyes looked up from the partially-dissected frog on her table. Seeing the three of them, she waved with the hand that held the scalpel. She held her left hand up rather awkwardly, with blood running from a gash in the middle of her palm. A thin stream of red trickled down to her elbow and dripped on the floor. "Hi!" She gave them a bright smile.

Nodding a quick greeting to the captain, she focused on the new arrivals. "You must be Jam and Ping!" She put down the scalpel and came over to shake their hands. Fortunately, the flow of blood seemed to have slowed enough so that it no longer dripped. "I've been so looking forward to meeting you."

For the first time, the woman evidenced awareness of something wrong with her left hand and eyed the wound. "I was hoping to get you to tell stories about your time on the BrainTrust, but I suppose I should introduce you to my mother and go get someone to look at this." Her eyes went wide. "Oh, by the way, I'm Ciara, the Mission Commander for the Prometheus archipelago. Ciara Thornhill."

They heard footsteps coming into the room, and Ciara looked past them to see who was coming. "And there's my mom now. Hey, Mom, Jack just brought us Jam and Ping!"

A well-kept woman in her fifties with carefully-styled brown hair and a slight smile stopped and scrutinized them. Her eyes froze when she saw Ciara's hand. She spoke in a commanding tone as befitted any good mother. "Ciara, you're bleeding all over the floor. You need to go get that seen to."

Ciara rolled her eyes. "Yes, Mother." She looked at Ping and Jam. "I guess Mom will tell you about the schools and the missions." She looked at her hand again, and for just a moment winced in irritated pain. "I should be back in a few." With that, she departed.

Ping watched with delight as she disappeared into the passage. "Oh, we are *so* going to get along. Just exceptionally well."

Jam groaned. "I'm afraid so."

The captain, who had been watching all of this with simple bemusement, realized he needed to perform some introductions. "Jam, Ping, this is Lenora Thornhill, Mission Commander for the Fuxing archipelago."

Jam added, "And, let's not forget, Ciara's mother."

Lenora raised an eyebrow. "Yes, by all means, let us not forget that."

Capt. Ainsworth left them, muttering that he had to get some real work done and he'd already had the lecture. Lenora led them through the passages rendered with lush forests to a conference room unlike any on the original BrainTrust. On the BrainTrust, the decorative deck themes ended when you entered the rooms, but in this conference room, the Lothlorien theme extended everywhere.

Except that whereas the passages were all at Lothlorien ground-level, the conference room was painted as if it were a treehouse. The floor appeared to be composed of living tree limbs, with uncovered patches that looked far down to the ground. Ping gasped in delight and started hopping from tree limb to tree limb around the table before she sat down. Jam put one foot tentatively on a patch of the floor that looked like air. Once she was convinced a solid floor lay beneath her, she thumped determinedly into a seat.

Lenora waved her hand at one of the rough wooden walls, and it turned into a wallscreen presenting an old, worn book in the middle of a flat white background. It was a hardback book with a red binding and an olive-drab cover, a small sailing ship in black and white in the center and the title *McGuffey's First Eclectic Reader*. "The field of education has hardly evolved since McGuffey published this volume two centuries ago. Children still come to school too early in the morning, before their brains are really awake. They read their books, listen to their teachers repeat the same things their teachers have said every year for the previous decade, and take the same test as all the other students in the same class at the same time. They work at the same pace in the same groove as everyone else. For our archipelagos to succeed, we must do radically better."

Ping stared in open-mouthed astonishment and Jam blinked, then commented, "I feel as if we've stepped into the middle of a conversation. What does replacing the McGuffey readers have to do with the success of the archipelagos?"

A head with sea-green hair poked into the room. Ciara looked at the book on the wallscreen. "Let me guess. Mom jumped to the 'radically better' part of the presentation without mentioning the immense hurdle we have to overcome."

Jam looked appreciatively at Ciara. "Precisely."

Ciara hopped into a chair, her left hand waving in the air, a thick white bandage wrapped around the palm. Someone had wiped the blood from her arm, though a spot of it still graced her elbow. "Mom, let me explain this part." She looked at Jam and Ping. "The BrainTrust, as you know, exploited the opportunity afforded by Deportation Phase II to take on board a high-density collection of brilliant, creative people who were already highly educated, extremely well-trained, and proven to be determined in the pursuit of new and valuable technologies. They already knew what to do and had the tools to do it, they just needed a home where they could pursue their goals without interference."

Ciara's mother stepped in. "But we've been there and done that. Now we have to dig deeper."

Ciara glared at her mother. "Shush." She looked back once again at Jam and Ping. "As Mom said, we're going to have to work harder. The people we want are the ones who have the characteristics to achieve great success but who don't have the opportunity because of poverty, culture, and political oppression."

Ping jumped from her chair. "No *hukou!*" She pounded her fist on the table, making Lenora's tablet jump. She hunched her shoulders sheepishly, as if, contrary to her nature, she was embarrassed by her outburst.

Ciara gave Ping a fist pump. "Got it in one."

Jam looked at both of them as if they had gone crazy.

Ping laughed. "*Hukou* is the system of mass human

registration used by the Chinese government to maintain control. A specific and particularly vile aspect of the system is that it splits the people of China into two castes: urban residents who have many privileges and opportunities, and rural peasants who're expected to remain rural peasants and work on the farms and die in the mines for the benefit of the urban caste. It's all hereditary. The only way you can get urban papers is to show direct lineage back to an urban dweller at the time Mao Zedong set it all up."

Ciara continued excitedly, "With over a billion people in the country, there are literally millions of people who would be classified as geniuses, trapped on farms plowing the fields, and in the mines inhaling toxic dust. Mom is going to fill the Fuxing with the best and brightest of them." She looked more soberly at Ping. "You and I are going to try to do approximately the same thing off the coast of Africa, which will be even harder because the disease levels are so much higher and the education levels are even lower."

Lenora stepped in as if on cue. "And that is why a radical advance in education is necessary. We must accelerate the education of the people we bring on board so they can become contributors to the pool of BrainTrust tech—engineers and innovators and creators of whole new businesses and industries—as quickly as humanly possible." She pointed back at the McGuffey reader on the display. "The McGuffey reader was revolutionary in its day. But the time for the next revolution has come." She went to a corner table where a small stack of tablets sat. "Jam, Ping, it's easier to experience than to explain." She synced one tablet to the left half of the wallscreen and the other to the right half. "You are about to work through a sample module from our Accel Educational Framework." She handed the tablets to the two new students.

The tablets had the same starting position. Each was situated at the beginning of a module about supply and demand under the heading of economics. Lenora explained, "In this version of the supply and demand module, we open with a short scenario, a game if you will, for the students to play. As it happens, this one is derived from a true life story from early in the century, when the Russians attempted to corner the market in uranium. In our scenario, they actually manage to buy all of the existing uranium mines. Needless to say, when they first got control they raised their prices. But then..."

Ping and Jam were already working the problem. Jam started creating new uranium mines to exploit the new price, which caused the supply to rise, which caused the price to fall, stabilizing at a point somewhat lower than the price had been at the beginning due to the presence of a significant surplus.

Ciara watched with amusement. "As you are already discovering, the Accel modules are loaded with addictive reinforcement features from gameplaying apps, to ensure they keep the student's attention. When children 'go to school' using Accel, they don't have to be dragged off to their rooms to do their homework. Rather, they have to be dragged out of their rooms to have something to eat."

Lenora corrected her daughter. "Actually, the software forces the students to take a break from time to time. The software can detect when the student is tiring and becoming less capable of retaining their lessons. So the student maximizes his time at maximum capability. And the instructional scaffolding built by the modules moderates the cognitive load so that that maximum capability, but no more, is continuously engaged."

Ping was barely listening. Instead of building more uranium mines like Jam, she had invested in engineering to develop a new line of nuclear reactors that used thorium rather than uranium. On the plot on her screen, the price of uranium started to fall and continued to fall. A new module appeared on her tablet describing the economic principle of substitution, when an overpriced commodity is replaced by new technology in the face of rising prices.

Lenora pointed at the differences between Jam's and Ping's screens. "Each student is able to learn in their own way, at their own pace, so you don't have a classroom forced to move at the speed of the slowest or most average child in the class. A precocious student can work through years of education in months, held back only by their own abilities."

Jam tore her eyes away from her tablet. "It must've cost a fortune to develop all these modules."

Lenora waved her hand. "In one sense it's worse than you think. If a student has trouble with a module, the software redirects the student into another module that covers the same material but in a different learning style. Simple examples are top-down learning and bottom-up learning, although our factor analysis has identified many different optimal learning strategies for different students on different topics. So the total number of modules that have been incorporated into Accel is vastly larger than any one student will ever see. But we didn't have to pay for them."

Ping finally looked up from having crushed the uranium monopolists in her scenario. "Free labor?" She sounded skeptical.

Lenora smiled. "Royalties."

Ciara explained, "Accel is not actually an educational tool. Rather, it's a framework for incorporating educational tools, mostly modules, and paying royalties to the authors based on the frequency with which those modules successfully teach students the specified material." Ciara eyed her mother. "Mom's a teacher. She designed Accel, but dad's a software engineer. He and Dr. James Caplan, the third founder of the company, implemented the first version of the framework and the first versions of the tools used to create and integrate new modules." She shook her head sadly. "Talk about a victim of your own success. Dad loved developing software, but now he's trapped on the BrainTrust running the Accel corporation, managing a bunch of former computer game developers and subject matter experts who get to do all the fun stuff."

Jam looked thoughtfully between the mother and the daughter. "So Accel has been a big success? It seems like it should be. After all, it frees the teachers to focus on helping the students who have problems, and lets some of the best teachers make money writing modules."

Ciara looked downcast.

Lenora pursed her lips. "Before coming to the Brain-Trust, we had some limited success with homeschooling parents. But for school system adoption, we ran into the usual problems with textbook publishers, teachers unions, and government certifying boards, each of whom would lose out if we shifted to a system that empowered each individual child to self-actualize at their own maximum speed."

Lenora raised her arms to the skies of Lothlorien. "We've known since the beginning of the century that children learn more, better, and faster if they start school later in the day. The research evidence has been overwhelming for decades, and *still* the vast majority of schools require their students to assemble and sit in their chairs and start listening to lectures at eight in the morning. For a society with school systems so rigid they can't even embrace a reasonable start time, what chance does a true revolution have?"

Ping's eyes gleamed. "So you're going to accelerate impoverished children from the backwaters of China through an educational experience that will make them better faster, and you're going to stick your success in their eyes."

Lenora hesitated, clearly wanting a more tactful description of the plan.

Ciara's eyes gleamed back. "You got it in one."

Meanwhile, Lenora flicked the display to a map of China with thousands of bright little dots. "We developed and deployed a testing module—psychological tests and measurements, really—available free for download. It does a first-pass screening for people with the intelligence, drive, etc., to become high-productivity BrainTrust members. Each dot represents someone who passed the tests. As you can see, they come literally from all over the map. We are going to make Mao's adage, "Let a hundred flowers blossom' into a reality the likes of which he could not have imagined." Her smile turned wicked. "And of which I suspect he would have mightily disapproved."

Jam heard the subtext. "He's not the only one who'll disapprove. There's a whole government bureaucracy—"

Ciara augmented this description. "The biggest, most cumbersome, and corrupt bureaucracy on Earth, in the country that first perfected bureaucracy thousands of years ago—"

Jam continued. "Dedicated to ensuring no one steps out of line or upsets the status quo."

Ciara leaned forward. "Backed by billions of surveillance cameras."

Ping added, "And millions of police, soldiers, and other thugs and enforcers."

Jam finished. "And led by a gang of tyrants no better than Mao. In fact, worse in many ways."

Lenora shrugged. "Exactly why we need people like you to take on the leadership of the expedition."

Jam just grunted.

Ping couldn't have cared less about the obstacles, risks, or problems. She whooped. "I'm in." Remembering that she was going off to fight pirates, she added, "Jam's in too."

Jam just grunted. Again.

5

SNATCHED

They that sow the wind shall reap the whirlwind.
  —Book of Hosea, Old Testament

Matt sat at the desk in his home office. He had surrendered to Gina's urging to buy Ben's abode on the *Haven* when he realized just how short of space they were throughout the BrainTrust. They'd had a hard time finding him a place to put his desk, much less a private conference room, on the *Argus* with his team, so he'd turned part of their new home into an office. The place was too large, in his opinion. Gina thought it a wee bit small, but she'd manage somehow.

Dash sat beside him, explaining some new opportunities to him. Somehow, opportunities always seemed like reasons to spend more money. He'd burned almost half the SpaceR cushion getting the *Heinlein* up and running. He'd have to be more careful in the future. Still, an opportunity was an opportunity.

Dash finished explaining how the methane converter

worked. "They've worked out the flaws in the prototypes they had before the launch. I think it is now ready."

Matt pursed his lips. "So you think I should buy one?" He tapped on his tablet, and the wallscreen shifted views. His leased LNG tanker sat snugly at anchor beside the *Hephaestus*, the modified isle ship where all the dangerous, toxic, or potentially explosive manufacturing was done. Both ships were parked a kilometer away from the main archipelago. "Will I be able to get rid of the tanker?"

Dash considered the question. "Probably not. You don't want to store the fuel for multiple launches on the *Heinlein*. If something goes wrong in the fuel-handling, it would be good if the explosion did not destroy the entire ship. Keeping the bulk of the fuel in a separate ship seems prudent."

Matt smiled. "Yes, prudent indeed."

Dash continued. "However, you could considerably reduce your fuel bills with locally-manufactured methane. Over half your fuel costs are carbon taxes. If you were converting algae, those costs would go away."

Matt nodded. "OK, now you're talking my language. So I buy a couple of these converters from the startup on *Dreams Come True*, and the savings go straight to the bottom line?"

Dash sighed. "It is not quite that easy. The BrainTrust artificial reef does not produce enough algae for your needs, and most of it is already dedicated to other purposes. We were able to handle a short emergency for your company, but it is not a long-term solution." She sat up straight and looked him in the eye. "You would need to build your own artificial reef."

Matt put his hands to his face and laughed. "And how much is *that* going to cost me?"

Dash did a short computation on her tablet. "You should talk with Alex yourself, but when he and I discussed it, we concluded it would cost comfortably less than a hundred million. In dollars, that is. Really, you should learn to deal with prices in SmartCoin like the rest of the people on the archipelago."

Disregarding this chastisement, Matt looked up at the ceiling as he did a rough estimate in his head. "So the payback time would be about three years."

"Indeed."

Matt sighed. "The numbers are still compelling."

"I thought you might consider them to be so." Dash looked at her tablet. "I have to go. I have real work to do on my own project." Her eyes lit up. "Though it is always a delight to help with the mission to conquer space."

Matt smiled back. "Thank you, Dash." He continued casually, "By the way, I thought I should mention that you are now a shareholder in SpaceR."

Dash shook her head in disbelief. "What?"

"I talked with the Board. You should be receiving confirmation in the next day or two. You're a shareholder." He smiled wickedly. "A substantial shareholder, at that. I want to tear you away from your other projects as often as I can."

"Goodness." She paused thoughtfully. "Does this make me a rocket scientist?"

"No. The work you did to earn the shares made you a rocket scientist."

Dash laughed briefly. "Of course. Thank you." She looked back at her tablet. "I really have to go."

As she departed, Matt's cell buzzed at him with the Darth Vader ringtone. He sighed. He had been dreading this conversation for days. He punched the answer button. "Good morning, Governor."

The Attorney General had been busy in the week since the governor had explained his proposal for forcing SpaceR back into line. Lining up the lawyers, the judge, and the police to enforce their newest edict, all in secret so SpaceR would have no chance to develop a defense, was exhausting. But it was done. Now he could relax and watch the wheels of Justice do their job. He listened, out of sight of the vidcam, as the governor spoke to Matthew Toscano. "I've been wanting to congratulate you on your successful launch."

"Thank you, Governor. I hope our change in launch venue does not change the excellent working relationship SpaceR has had with you."

The governor's smile fixed itself in place. The Attorney General was a little surprised he could not hear the governor's teeth grinding, but he still had control of the situation. "You owe us four billion dollars," he stated in a matter-of-fact tone used to state the obvious."

"Ah. Yes. I'm not surprised to hear that's your opinion."

The governor jerked. "It's not just a matter of opinion, it's a matter of law. We passed a law. It's the law. You have to obey the law."

"Governor, as you might expect, my legal team is already preparing a case to persuade the courts to throw out your law. If I can get it to the Supreme Court, I wouldn't be surprised if we win."

The Attorney General winced. The Supreme Court was stacked with Red lawyers. While the political dynamics for the Chief Advisor were complicated in this case, there was a real chance he would support SpaceR. The Supreme Court's ruling in that case would be a foregone conclusion.

But it would be far too late to help SpaceR, given the circumstances that were about to change. Right now.

The governor smiled. The Attorney General could see that the governor had not yet forgotten that he still had control of the conversation; he still had the power. "I'm sorry you feel that way." He lifted a phone dramatically as Matt and the Attorney General watched. "Commander, it's a go."

He put the phone down and looked back at Matt on the screen. "The California State Guard has just entered your SpaceR rocket factory in Hawthorne. It is hereby seized on behalf of the State of California." His smile grew broader. "Think of it as a mechanic's lien. Just pay your four billion, and of course, the additional penalty for failing to pay promptly. The troops will leave, and everything will be fine."

***

Matt felt a guilty sense of relief. He finally knew for sure what the governor would do. He wasn't surprised, actually. His management team had identified this as one of the low-probability possibilities—low probability because it wouldn't just hammer SpaceR, it would hammer the SpaceR union members, a force even the governor needed to reckon with.

Regardless, it was a catastrophe for the company, but at least it was now out in the open.

Matt knew that what he ought to do was to start negotiating. He didn't have the money anymore. He could pay maybe a billion now and the rest over time, but there were two problems with this. One problem was that it would never be over if he agreed now. The state of California had been talking for years about scoring an extra helping of direct income from the biggest companies' revenues. He had no doubt that that was the direction this conversation would soon take. Four billion now, and more and more for all eternity.

But that was not the reason Matt did not immediately begin a calm and deliberate negotiation. The real reason was that he was furious. Matt would not bow as if this jerk were a king.

Matt did the best he could under the circumstances. "We'll talk about this later," he choked out, then hung up.

He breathed deeply. He wondered idly if the Board would replace him now as they had so recently replaced his predecessor. But he realized he was probably safe. The Board knew as well as he did that any course of action other than the one he had taken was just a way to engage in slow suicide. They would leave him in place as long as he could figure out how to deal with this new crisis. All was not lost. He still had a couple of billion in working capital.

Matt already knew what to do, or at least what questions to ask; his contingency planning having progressed that far. He'd already rejected the idea of trying to move his manufacturing plant to SpaceR's facility in Texas. They had no manufacturing infrastructure there, neither equipment nor skilled personnel. It would take years to bring up a new plant there, and they didn't have the time. There was only one obvious solution. Maybe.

So Matt called Alex, the BrainTrust's chief engineer for the *Argus*. Alex answered the phone with, "I've been expecting you to call. We have the stabilizers in place. You should be able to take the *Heinlein* outside the reef for the next launch. We won't have to keep this crazy fleet config- uration with every ship sitting in a circle like they're in a seance."

"That's great, Alex. It'll be a relief to everyone to be able to walk between the ships again, rather than having to take a copter or a boat." Though Matt had to admit a couple of the boats, built by entrepreneurs when they saw the need for better transportation around the detached archipelago, were pretty cool. He had thought about buying one, but where would he get the time to sail it? Meanwhile, he had an emergency on his hands. Again. "But that's not why I'm calling. I have another emergency. I know the *Argus* is designed primarily as a ship for building ships. Have you ever thought about what it would take to build a rocket?"

Matt enjoyed thinking of himself as a people-reader of reasonably advanced powers. He was having trouble reading Dash, however, so he was excited about visiting her in her office. Would there be any hints he could glean about her personality from the pictures on her walls and the memorabilia on her desk?

Even before he entered the office, he found his first clue.

Beside the door, a sheet of yellow legal paper in an elegant gold frame hung like a painting. The sheet was covered in mathematical symbols written in sharp strokes of the pencil; a little wild, as if the author were working either in haste or in pain.

He saw Dash approach from the corner of his eye. She asked forlornly, "I don't suppose you can see what is wrong with these equations?"

He looked at it again. It had been a very long time since he'd done exotic math. He shook his head. "Sorry, it just looks like gibberish to me."

Dash sighed. "I just ask everyone who comes by and looks at it."

"I see."

Dash led him into the office. It was rather austere, but Matt thought she might have started the slow accumulation of memories that tended to fill a vacuum.

In a vertical column upon one wall were seven tiny photos of elderly people. Each had a number beneath it. He recognized Ben's photo with a zero beneath it. Photos below that had negative numbers, negative five thousand to negative ten thousand. Above Ben was a woman with a positive four thousand, and a man with a six thousand, and at the very top, numerically out of order, was a woman with a one and a plus sign beside it.

The bookcase held little in the way of books. There was

a legal pad, the top page of which was covered with the same kind of math he'd found outside. And there was a very thick sheaf of neatly stacked papers with an elegant black and gold pen sitting atop it.

Those were the closest things to books to be found in the bookcase, but other odd items struck him. On a lower shelf in the bookcase were the remains of an old-fashioned stethoscope. The rubber tubing seemed to have been cut from it, leaving only pieces. And on a high shelf, a pair of gleaming black lacquer sheaths held two Japanese swords, one long, one short.

Matt had a suspicion that he was seeing keys to the soul of his business associate—well, face it, she was now his friend—but the keys needed keys to unlock them. His curiosity would have to be quenched some other day. Today they had business. Emergency business.

Colin walked into the conference room on the *Argus*, mystified. "Didn't we just do this a couple of weeks ago?"

Dash watched him as he looked around the table at the usual suspects: Matt, Werner, Alex and her.

Matt looked up at Colin from the head of the table, an exhausted, rage-tinted expression on his face. "I take it you haven't heard the news from California."

Colin grabbed a chair and raised an eyebrow. "I take it your successful launch from the BrainTrust was not welcomed equally in all corners of the state?"

Werner snorted. "That bastard in the governor's mansion screwed us again."

Dash said, "Well, at least you have a little more time to respond this time."

Now Alex and Werner shared an exhausted look. Alex said, "Not as much as you'd think," and Werner finished, "for a much bigger job."

Matt explained the situation to Colin; it was his fourth repetition that day. "They've seized our factory in Hawthorne. No more new rockets until we hand over the four billion dollars." He continued wryly, "Half of which we don't have anymore because we gave it to you." He saw that Colin about to object, and corrected himself, "We used it to pay almost everyone on the BrainTrust for something or other."

Alex pushed the conversation back on topic. "So you want to build rockets out here on the BrainTrust."

Werner and Matt both nodded. Matt said, "I don't suppose you can just tweak the *Argus* to build rockets as well as ships? It seems like you manufacture everything else out here."

Alex shook his head. "The *Argus* can manufacture an amazing variety of objects and systems, but building the ships requires a lot of specialized gear. Quite different from the specialized gear you need to build a rocket, I suspect."

Dash entered an observation. "Even the materials are very different. The BrainTrust has spent over a decade evolving the science and technology to use local materials as much as possible. The graphene-reinforced carbon on your launch pad is a perfect example. It is made from pure carbon that is extracted from the reef." She pointed at the wallscreen, showing a real-time view of the *Heinlein* as it slowly motored away from the archipelago. "Your new launch ship has a hull made with a skeleton of magnesium alloy embedded in calcium carbonate that actually grows onto the skeleton, accreted from the seawater."

Matt looked puzzled. "Calcium carbonate? I've never heard of that being used as a building material. Or as anything else, for that matter."

Dash explained, "You may not have heard of it, but you are quite familiar with it. Seashells are made of calcium carbonate. A team on the *Dreams Come True* adapted the mechanism from sea life. The hulls of the newest isle ships grow in seawater in a manner somewhat similar to the way coral reefs grow."

Colin veered back to the general topic. "Carbon, magnesium, calcium carbonate, plastics made from methane—these are the strongly-preferred building materials here."

Dash continued, "Your boosters are made primarily with aluminum-lithium alloy. Lighter and stiffer than even pure aluminum, but utterly unlike anything we use here."

Alex nodded. "We have no tools at all for working with aluminum or its alloys. You're talking about a whole different ecosystem of technology."

Werner shook his head. "Wait a minute. I know you built the VATT for the *Heinlein* out of titanium, so you *do* work with other materials."

Alex explained, "Yes, we use a lot of titanium even though we have to import it. One of our sets of printers is designed for additive manufacturing with titanium, though a lot of our titanium is used just to plate the magnesium in situations where the magnesium could corrode."

Dash blew out a breath. "Could we make the booster bodies out of micro-honeycomb titanium?"

She looked at Werner. "When using a 3D printer for manufacturing, you can create shapes with intricate interiors as easily as shapes with solid cores. Micro-honeycomb titanium might have the weight and stiffness you need." She muttered as she tapped on her notebook, "I'd need to talk to a real expert to find out."

Matt looked astonished that Dash would need to consult with a "real expert" on anything, but he let it slide. He turned to Alex. "So, if Dash figures out a way to build the boosters at sea using some sort of materials she'll no doubt invent on the spot, do you have space to build them here on the *Argus*?"

Alex looked at Colin. "It's a big change from everything else we build. We're already way behind schedule on virtually everything planned before SpaceR's arrival."

Matt chuckled. "I just can't feel sorry for you. I'm sure you made a handsome profit off of me for that theft."

Colin confessed, "Oh, yes, we walloped you good. We now have plenty of money. But it takes a lot of time to turn money into production machinery, which is our current shortage."

Dash put her tablet down, upon which she had been tapping with intermittent fury. "My materials engineering friends think the titanium micro-honeycomb will work. Even with additive manufacturing you'll be using a lot of titanium so it will be expensive, but you should be able to get more launches per booster. I think in the long run, once we have the process down, you'll get a total life-cycle cost reduction."

Matt raised his eyes and his hands to the sky as if asking for deliverance. "How can it be that every damn thing on the BrainTrust costs more up front, but saves money in the long run? Couldn't we have something that was cheap up front, just once?"

Everyone laughed briefly. Colin spoke. "Half the reason these things are costing you so much is because of the emergency timelines. Once your situation settles down, your costs should fall appreciably."

Matt refocused. "OK, back to the key question. Titanium for the boosters. You're all set up for 3D printing with it. Can you build them on the *Argus*?"

Alex closed his eyes. The room hushed as everyone awaited his answer. Finally, he said reluctantly, "It would be best to build a new 3D printer. Something on a scale never before seen, that could print the whole booster as a single piece." He shook his head. "What's the diameter of the boosters?"

Dash answered instantaneously, "Three-point-seven meters, or twelve feet, for you Americans."

Alex shook his head. "We'd have to rip out a deck. The printer will have to be two decks high. You'd be better off building a new ship." He looked at Matt. "How much time do we have?"

Matt's shoulders drooped. "As you know, we have six Kestrel Heavies here. The average booster has about ten launches left in its lifecycle. We can maybe stretch that a bit, but we launch almost every day. We have two months before things go sour."

The silence was so thick Dash could have cut it with her scalpel. Colin asked, "What about your other three

MARC STIEGLER

launch facilities in Texas? They're running on borrowed time as well."

Matt ran his hand through his hair. "They're in better shape than we are here. They have about five months of flight capacity before their last booster needs to retire."

Dash followed Colin's lead. "So, if we could move two Kestrel Heavies, with an average of ten launches per rocket, we'd gain another month."

Werner pointed out the obvious. "But at the cost of accelerating the day when we can't launch at all."

Alex sighed. "In three months we might be able to do something. We'll need full blueprints of the current Kestrel Heavy, of course. And we'll need as many subcomponents as you can get elsewhere, either onshore manufacturing or recycling from the spent boosters."

He pulled out his tablet and started muttering. "We'd want to rip up the *Argus* enough to make two double-height decks, one for building the new cores, one for scavenging the still-usable parts out of the old cores. We'll need a list of all the things other than the cores that we need, and develop plans for importing or making them all. What other thing are there? The second stages, the payload fairings, and the payload capsules are obvious ones. I suspect we are nowhere near being able to manufacture the crewed capsules." He rolled his head from side to side. "The engines. Lots of the engine plumbing can be printed in-place with the fuselages, but I need a list of all the parts that can't."

Werner waved the problem away. "If you can build the first-stage boosters, I think you'll find the second stage straightforward. We can contract with someone in a Red state to make the fairings, and the capsules have long life-times." He paused. "We have enough engines stored in a warehouse in Texas for one more Kestrel Heavy if we can get them here."

Matt listened with a rising sense of anxiety. "Can you really do this? When I think about how long it would take to build an entire rocket-manufacturing center from scratch back in Hawthorne, I find it almost impossible to believe you can pull this off. Recognizing the irony, of course, that I'm the one who was foolish enough to ask if it were possible. We couldn't even bring up another assembly line in our current Hawthorne factory, with all the infrastructure already in place, in this time frame."

Colin addressed his concern. "Don't let dirtside timetables and schedules distort your perspective too much, Matt. Remember, general-purpose bots are completely legal here. They work twenty-four hours a day, seven days a week. Depending on the job needing to be done, we're looking at a factor of five increase in speed. Even a factor of ten, if a streamlined regulatory structure makes a difference. If you could do it in a year in California, we can probably do it here in three months."

Colin took a deep breath. "We're going to have to figure out how to parallelize this project with the shipbuilding or the Board will never go for it. Alex, I realize that building the superstructures for new ships will have to be put on hold—this whole ship is going to be dedicated to the rebuild for punching out the boosters—but can we at least lay down skeletons and start growing the hulls for two or three ships? Since the reactors are built on the *Hephaestus*, their assembly shouldn't be impacted. Once we have the hulls, can we bring their reactors online, and get them ready to install the decks and superstructures once we have some capacity again?"

Matt looked once more to the heavens. "I can't believe I'm going to say this, but if you're laying down hulls, lay another one for me too. I can already see I'll need another isle ship." When everyone stared at him, he explained, "I'm going to have to bring my workers out here, aren't I? At the end of the day it's all going to be here, right?"

Alex laughed low in his chest. "We've already got one framework in the water. I guess I'll put down two more hulls while we're rushing around like chickens with our heads cut off. Even if Matt decides in the end not to take one, I suspect we'll find a use for it."

Colin joined in the laughter. "I suspect so." He paused. "The Board is not going to love this, profitable though it may be. As Alex already pointed out, this will play holy hell with our existing schedules." He smiled at Matt. "But I think it will be profitable."

Matt just put his face in his hands and groaned.

6

EASY CRUISING

For every complex problem there is an answer that is clear, simple, and wrong.
  —H.L. Mencken

Dash and Chance stepped onto the small-ship dock of the *Haven*. Dmitri's yacht was unmistakable. It was, as Dmitri had promised, by far the largest. Dash counted five decks. She suspected the flat empty space at the stern of the top deck was a copter pad.

But the item that confirmed this was the *Buccaneer* was the sight of Dmitri himself standing at the stern, a deck above them, waving. He looked quite spiffy in his denim jacket and a Breton Stripe t-shirt.

Dash waved back. "There he is," she said, pointing.

Chance yelled, "Ahoy!" and picked up speed.

Dmitri met them at the gangway. "Welcome," he said with delight. He pointed at a box with a couple of pairs of shoes in it. He was barefoot.

The night before, Dash had read on the web about mega-yacht etiquette, so she slipped off her sandals and dropped them in the box. Chance kicked her flipflops neatly into the zone.

As they walked up the gangway Dash hitched up her sarong to give her legs more freedom of movement. The sarong had been a clothing choice compromise she'd reached with Chance. Dash had planned to wear blue jeans and a leather jacket. Chance, who'd read the same yacht etiquette pages as she had, said this was not acceptable. They should wear bathing suits, she'd asserted. After all, the yacht had both a hot tub and a swimming pool. Dash countered that she was not about to run around virtually unclothed, wearing nothing but a swimsuit.

In the end, Dash had worn the swimsuit underneath a sarong tied over her shoulders, covering her from neck to ankle. Chance had conceded and worn a similar sarong, though she draped hers from one shoulder. Chance had gotten a wicked gleam in her eye when she'd told Dash that they'd have to ditch the sarongs to get into the hot tub. Dash had not replied. She had no intention of getting in the pool or the tub or taking off the sarong under any circumstances whatsoever.

They stepped onto an aft platform with chairs and a table. A small boat sat in a cradle; a dinghy Dash thought, though it was not immediately clear how you would get it into the water.

The gangway automatically retracted, and Dmitri spoke. "Let me show you around as we get underway." A bot unhitched the line holding them to the dock, and the ship slipped smoothly away from the *Haven*.

Together, the three of them walked into the main body of the ship, to be greeted by two more people. Dmitri spoke, "Dash, I think you already know Gleb and Yefim. Gleb, Yefim, this is Chance." Gleb and Yefim had not been with Dmitri on the day he showed up on the *Chiron* and invited the two of them, quite insistently, aboard his mega-yacht. Dash still wasn't quite sure how she had wound up agreeing to go, though Chance's enthusiastic acceptance and consequent assistance to Dmitri in his pleadings had much to do with it.

As greetings went all around the group, Dash noted sourly that Gleb and Yefim had both been allowed to wear deck shoes, jeans, and leather jackets.

As Dmitri led the way toward the fore of the ship, he showed off the mahogany and gold decor, put together, he explained, by the Pierrejean Design Studio of Paris. The movie theater, with seating for twelve, had lounge recliners for seats. If the movie playing were subpar, Dash suspected you could easily fall asleep there.

Eventually, they took a staircase up a level and headed aft into a piano bar. "Drinks?" Dmitri asked.

Dash smiled. "A Coke, please." She steeled herself for ribbing about her choice of drink, but Dmitri just poured her Coke into a gold-rimmed glass.

"Chance?"

"Scotch on the rocks," she requested.

Dmitri smiled, "A woman after my own heart."

He took them aft once more, and they settled into curved sofas around a coffee table in the salon. Both port and starboard walls held enormous windows. To port, they could see the isle ships, and to starboard, they could see the lush green kelp interspersed with an occasional sandy beach that marked the artificial reef encircling the archipelago.

Dash spoke with a joy that surprised her. "It's beautiful."

Dmitri sat a little straighter and prouder. "My yacht, the isle ships, or the reef?"

"All of them."

Yefim and Gleb had settled in opposite corners, and Dash realized they hadn't seen another soul during the tour. "Where is everyone else? Don't you have a crew?"

Dmitri waved the question away. "Not really. Most of the work is done by the general-purpose bots. Illegal in both America and the Russian Union, of course, but not here with the BrainTrust." He sighed. "Alexei and Vasily, my other two assistants, are around here somewhere, but the only other person on board is my captain, who doubles as a pilot, navigator, and bot wrangler."

Chance had been fully absorbed in looking at and touching everything they passed. "Sounds like he has more than a fulltime job."

Dmitri laughed. "Sometimes."

Dash, who had been watching the reef slip past them, frowned. "Dmitri, aren't we getting awfully close to the reef? Are we going into the channel? Were you planning on taking us outside the reef into the open ocean?"

Dmitri seemed to tense. "Yes, I thought you'd enjoy a view of the BrainTrust from a little farther away. It's quite a sight."

Now Dash pushed herself forward from the excessively comfortable couch. "We cannot do that. Colin says I must never go beyond the reef, or I will be, uh, 'fair game.'"

Dmitri cleared his throat. "Not to worry. There's a Russian cruiser out there too, you know. The Americans can't get you here."

Now Dash rose in alarm. "Do not do this, Dmitri." She pulled out her tablet and watched as Dmitri stared at it in surprise. She thought smugly that he was wondering, *where had she been keeping that?* But he should have known she'd never be without it.

She had no signal. "You're jamming my wifi!"

Now Dmitri, Gleb, and Yefim were all on their feet. Dmitri held up his hand. "Just stay calm. Everything will be all right."

Chance leaped up as well. While Chance quietly scanned the opposition, Dash cried, "What are you doing!"

Dmitri winced. "I'm taking you to the Premier. As you may know, he, like the American President, has a rather desperate need for rejuvenation. He's putting together the finest laboratory in all of Russia for you." He glanced at Chance. "You too. You'll both be treated like royalty. You just have to help the Premier with this little problem of aging."

Dash stared at him with a mix of bewilderment and rage. "I thought you hated the Premier."

Dmitri nodded. "Very much so. But it's complicated."

Toni felt her eyes burning as she peered into the high-resolution hologram of a scramjet engine she and her two partners were designing. It would be fun, she thought idly, to whip up a miniature version on the printers in the *Argus* just to see if it worked.

But the BrainTrust would probably frown on testing it any place closer than the *Hephaestus*. Too much effort.

She looked up at the wallscreen displaying a view of the ocean from the archipelago out to the reef. Jet skis raced along, leaving foaming white wakes, while a couple of homebrew copters danced above the waves. In the left corner of the screen, she could see the *Haven* sticking out like a finger from the main body of ships. She recognized Dmitri's yacht docked there...and she could barely make out Dmitri himself, waving at someone walking down the dock toward him.

Dash? And Chance! They were too far to recognize their faces, but she could not mistake Chance's tattoos.

And they were getting on the yacht! Damnation! Dash still didn't understand how dangerous the people were who wanted her and her just-telomeres-that-are-not-a-fountain-of-youth therapy.

And Dash had barely gotten on board when the yacht's bots tossed away the docking lines, and the *Buccaneer* accelerated away.

Toni dropped her holographic editing pen on the bench, muttered an apology, and took off running for the *Argus*.

Toni had flown a number of the copters scattered around the BrainTrust, somewhat sating her urge to fly even if she couldn't break the sound barrier. Lately, she'd been lusting to try out Matt's new copter, reputed to be the fastest thing in the fleet. She smiled grimly. It looked like she finally had an excuse to check it out.

She reached the copter bay on the *Argus* in record time. Fortunately, the *Argus* was adjacent to *BTU*. She hooked her tablet to the public external cameras to see where the *Buccaneer* was. As she had feared, from the size and direction of the wake it looked like the yacht was steaming full regulation speed toward the southeastern channel through the reef. As she watched, it cleared the area where jet skis roamed and accelerated.

Tori slewed the display's view to look beyond the reef. The Russian cruiser that had been shadowing the American ever since Assault Night was breaking away, heading toward the reef. Tori was suddenly quite certain that her worst fears were true. She pounded on her tablet to connect with Dash, but to no avail; Dmitri had undoubtedly jammed the comms. She texted Colin.

Dash on Dmitri's yacht. Sailing beyond reef. Russian cruiser coming.

She ran to the beautifully-streamlined silver copter with a cherry red racing stripe. A teenager was polishing it lovingly. "Out of the way," she demanded. "Emergency."

The kid launched himself in front of her. "Wait a minute! It's my copter!" He looked away. "Well, it's Mr. Toscano's, but I designed it."

Toni changed her plan on the spot. "Great. Get in. We have to rescue Dash."

The kid's eyes widened. "Dr. Dash?"

"Yes, that Dash. Is there another one?"

He looked doubtful. "I don't think Mr. Toscano will be happy if we take his copter."

Toni growled, "He'll be even less happy if Dash, his top tech advisor, gets kidnapped."

The teenager's eyes widened even more. He turned and started to climb into the pilot's seat.

"Move over," Toni commanded. "I'll be flying."

The teenager's expression turned stubborn, but he was overruled by a hard shove. He yelped and dropped into the passenger's seat.

Toni looked over the cockpit. "Dual controls. Good. You'll be taking over in a bit."

This seemed to mollify the boy. Toni lit up the engines, and they shot out of the bay like they were on fire.

Dash rubbed her arms and paced back and forth in the absurdist ostentation of the lounge, where she was imprisoned in mahogany-and-gold luxury. On top of everything else, she felt naked wearing the sarong instead of her lab coat. Never again, she promised herself. "You cannot get away with this, Dmitri," she stated again carefully, as if speaking to a naughty child.

"It certainly seems like I'll get away with it at the moment," he replied with a note of surprise. "Of course, that probably means something is about to go wrong." He shrugged. "But I'm Russian. We expect things to go wrong."

Dash stopped pacing and just stared at him. "Take us home before it is too late."

He shook his head. "I fear you couldn't possibly understand. The only way out of this for me is forward." He waved his hands at his two goons. "Gleb and Yefim will stay to keep you company. They work for me." He shuddered. "Unlike Alexei and Vasily, whom I will keep elsewhere." He turned to Gleb. "Do not let them leave this room. It's not safe outside."

Gleb nodded, and Dmitri departed.

Chance, meanwhile, seemed to be taking this whole kidnapping with unnatural calm. She tried to stretch her leg up onto the back of a chair. The sarong wrapped around her leg, restraining her motion. "Dash, you were right all along, these sarongs are awfully confining." She shrugged. "Well, might as well get comfortable."

Chance untied her sarong, dropped it casually on the floor, and walked to the refrigerator wearing her bikini. Dash couldn't understand how she could walk around like that so unselfconsciously. It must have been because of her time as a model. Chance asked, "I don't suppose we can go to the pool?"

Yefim was watching her admiringly. "I'm afraid not," he said, truly remorseful.

Chance pulled beers from a small refrigerator in the back. "Dash? You want one?" As Dash shook her head, Chance continued, "Of course not. Gleb? Yefim?" She turned from the refrigerator with two beers. Both of the guards shook their heads regretfully. Chance shook her head. "Cowards," she muttered as she put down one beer, popped the top off the other, and raised it to her lips. She threw her head back and gulped loudly, though it seemed to Dash, scrutinizing her with suspicious astonishment, that she didn't actually swallow much beer.

Chance was gliding through the room toward Yefim when they heard gunfire outside. Dash and both guards looked quickly toward the door. Dash saw a flicker of movement where Chance was approaching Yefim, then there was a sharp thump, followed by a much louder thud. Looking toward the sound, she saw Yefim crumpled on the ground.

Chance shrieked, "Yefim!" and jumped in shock. She knelt next to Yefim, then stood again. "Dash, something's wrong with Yefim!"

Dash rushed to them, briefly wondering, not what was wrong with Yefim, but rather what was wrong with Chance. Chance had never acted squeamish before, and she certainly had the skills to do a preliminary assessment of an unconscious person and apply first aid.

Meanwhile, Gleb approached them slowly as Dash bent over the unconscious man.

Dash discovered Yefim's problem with a few seconds of examination. "Severe blunt force trauma to the—"

Another sharp *thump* followed by a much louder *thud* interrupted her. Dash swallowed a squeak as Gleb's body hit the floor just behind her. She swiftly inspected the left side of his head. "Severe blunt trauma to the head. Again." She looked up at Chance sternly, and Chance looked back with beatific innocence.

Forcing down an expression that tried to turn mirthful, Dash observed, "He seems to be alive, in all events."

Chance nodded. "Of course. I used Cro Cop's head kick. It can kill, but I used my right leg." When Dash just stared at her, she sighed. "Never mind. It's an MMA joke."

"MMA? The videos you were in?"

"Yeah."

"I thought they liked your tattoos."

"Oh, they did. I had the best tattoos of any of the women fighters."

"Aha, so you *were* a fighter. One of the top three in the world, no doubt."

Chance laughed. "Not hardly." She shrugged, looking a little embarrassed. "Fourth in Arizona." She paused. "I might have made it into the top two, but I didn't enjoy hurting people."

Dash's eyes widened as she looked meaningfully, first at Gleb, then at Yefim.

Chance coughed. "I said I didn't like hurting *people*. This was different."

Dash frowned again, but then a gleam came into her eyes. "Our friends here have undoubtedly experienced concussions." She pulled off her sarong and used her teeth to rip off several strips of silk. She moved swiftly to tie their hands, gag them, and blindfold them. "The prescribed treatment for concussion is extended bed rest. Avoid both physical and mental exertion."

Chance nodded. "I agree with your prescription," she declared. "I believe the bindings will help them avoid physical agitation, and the blindfolds will assist in keeping their minds calm by reducing sensory input." She gave Dash a thumbs-up. "Brilliant, Doctor."

"We do what we can with the resources available," Dash offered, as though speaking to a room full of students.

"May we depart now that their treatment is in place?"

"I believe so." Dash grabbed her sadly ripped sarong and wrapped it around her hips. It did not cover her as well as before, but it was better than nothing. "Swiftly."

So they trotted toward the door at the far end of the salon whence they had entered, going deeper into the ship.

Toni struggled for a few moments as the high-powered copter tried to get away from her. The kid kept giving her strangled instructions, knowing not to scream but desperately wanting to.

Finally, she had control, and they streaked over the BrainTrust to home in on the *Buccaneer*. The yacht was already through the channel and outside the reef. In the distance, Toni could see the Russian cruiser cutting the water as it approached. The American cruiser, no doubt mystified by this sudden change in the behavior of a ship that had previously paralleled her every move, decided something must be up, so she was charging along behind. The California Coastal Patrol ships and the two Chinese frigates accompanying them continued to follow their orders and dutifully followed the American.

Toni muttered, "What a mess" as she arrowed toward the yacht. She growled at the kid, "What's your name?"

"Ted," he replied, "Ted Simpson."

"OK, Ted, here's how it's going to go down." Toni pointed at the yacht. "You see that copter pad on the back there?"

Ted nodded.

"We're going to do a touch and go, but with a twist. I'm going to touch and jump out, and you're going to go. Got it?"

Ted nodded. "Uh, yeah."

Somebody trotted out of the cabin onto the deck just forward of the copter pad. He carried an AK-47. Toni veered hard left as the man raised the machine gun to his shoulder and began firing.

Ted gasped.

Toni shouted, not meaning to, "You're buckled in, right?"

"Uh, right."

"OK, new plan. The copter pad has been compromised. That's the military way of saying, we just got fucked. You with me?"

Ted nodded.

"OK, so we're going to zip around the port side here and do a touch and go on that roof over the second or third deck towards the bow. While we're zipping, you're going to keep an eye out for more guys with guns. Got it?"

"Yes, ma'am." Ted seemed to have steadied himself, and he started scanning the ship with new intensity. The man on the copter pad was still shooting, occasionally pausing to pop in a new magazine.

"When we get to the roof, it'll be a really touchy touch. I doubt the roof can take the full weight of the copter. We don't want to crash through, right?"

Ted shook his head. "No, ma'am."

"Then you're going to take the copter out several hundred meters and start circling the ship. Zig and zag and pop and drop to keep them guessing. Got it?"

Ted swallowed hard. "Got it." Suddenly he smiled. "Jinking. Just like laser tag, only for real."

Toni grinned wolfishly. "Just like laser tag."

Dash and Chance found themselves wandering like lost children in the mansion of an evil witch. From the salon, they'd passed through the piano bar, and trotted hastily past the circular staircase that Dash was pretty sure Dmitri had used when he had left them.

Beyond the staircase Dash paused; the med bay was on the port side. She could not help herself—she stuck her head in to see what Dmitri had for emergency first aid. A quick scan, and Dash muttered, "Unbelievable. So much boat, so little preparation for the unforeseen." She ran in, opened a couple of drawers, and came back out. "Not even a scalpel to be found. This must be improved upon." They continued onward.

Eventually, they found themselves in a small room with two chairs set to look out the wraparound windows overlooking the bow. A quick glance told them the situation was still evolving. The Russian cruiser was heading toward them, tailed by the entire little fleet of naval antagonists. A small California Coastal Patrol yacht, apparently a hydrofoil, had kicked up its speed and was racing past the American cruiser in a determined effort to reach and pass the Russian.

"This is not good," Chance stated the obvious.

Dash frowned. "Let us see if we can find Dmitri."

Chance stared at her. "And then what?"

Dash smiled. "And then we persuade him to choose a wiser path."

Chance smiled back. She had just started leading back the way they'd come when they heard gunfire. Chance hesitated. "What's that?"

Dash pushed her gently forward, and they picked up

speed. "I believe it's the thing going wrong that Dmitri had been expecting. How do you say it in American Westerns?"

"'Here comes the cavalry?'"

Dash nodded. "Precisely."

Ted shouted, "There's another guy with a gun." Calming a little, he added, "Down on a lower deck, amidships."

"Good," Toni replied. "He can't shoot through the ship to hit us when we touch down."

And so it was. Toni touched down and jumped out. Ted lifted away and Toni rolled to her feet, then ran.

She'd been thinking about the tactical situation while driving the copter and had concluded that the strategic key was the bridge. If she could take the helm and turn the ship back to the BrainTrust, she'd have more time to deal with everything else. Two guys outside with guns, surely more inside with Dash, and Dmitri someplace. Grab Dmitri and offer a trade?

The bridge was two decks above her, just in front of the copter pad. The front of the bridge had no entrance, just glass. You had to enter the bridge from an internal staircase or from the pad. As she raced around the starboard side to hopefully avoid the gunman on the port side, she wondered if the gunman who had been on the pad was still there.

There was no real exterior deck here, but the streamlined and sloping sides supplied adequate traction for her running shoes. Thus she came silently upon the copter pad from a direction no one would expect.

And there he was, watching Ted buzz by; Vasily was his name, if she remembered correctly from the party. The gunner seemed unable to decide whether to spend more ammo firing at the copter. Just as well, since Ted was uncomfortably close, but the boy did make a great distraction.

Toni was behind Vasily before the bastard had any clue she was there. She hooked a foot in front, pushed him forward, and tried to remember her Krav Maga instructor's words. *Keep your fingers apart and strike at an angle. This way you have a greater probability of making contact with his eyes. Make sure your fingers are hard and strong while striking.* Ah, yes. She remembered now.

The gunman tripped and fell. She spread her fingers as specified and let his own falling weight drive his eye into her middle finger. By the time he hit the deck he was no longer interested in the proceedings, being literally half-blind. He squeezed the grip of his gun convulsively, tapped the trigger, and grazed his own chest and shoulder with a burst of bullets, leaving a light jet of blood spewing across the deck. Toni put a knee in his back, reached underneath, and wrested the weapon from the gunman who, as her instructor might have said, had lost situational awareness. She smacked his head against the deck a couple of times just to be sure.

AK-47 in hand, Toni charged through the back door onto the bridge. Except it wasn't the bridge. It was an elegant conference room, with an elegant mahogany table, perfectly circular, eight chairs all set like they were ready for the Knights of the Round Table. It seemed unlikely to Toni that Dmitri used this room often. He didn't seem like a Round Table-style of leader. She rushed into the next room.

She'd found the bridge at last. A man in a perfectly-tailored captain's uniform looked back at her.

"Turn the ship around," she ordered.

"Ma'am, Mikhailov would not—"

Toni fired a three-round burst through the window by the captain's head. "Turn the ship around."

"Yes, ma'am."

Dash had insisted on making a detour before taking the staircase to find Dmitri, so they had gone back into the piano bar and turned right into a starboard-side dining room. A china cabinet sat in one corner. Dash rifled the drawers and drew out a gleaming silver prize. "A steak knife!" she exclaimed. She held it up, letting the light reflect in all directions. Like everything else on the yacht, it was as beautiful as it was functional. "Not as sharp or well-balanced as my scalpel, but not bad."

Chance's eyes widened. "You're planning to use that on Dmitri?"

Dash dropped her hand to hold the knife by her side. "Of course not."

Chance looked at the knife thoughtfully. "Even so, could you *threaten* to use the knife?"

Dash gripped the knife hard and gave Chance her fiercest, most threatening expression.

Chance covered her mouth to cover bubbling laughter.

After she recovered, she suggested practically, "We'll persuade him some other way."

They heard heavy footsteps outside, quickly drowned by an engine, and froze. Looking out the long window, they could see Alexei running toward them. Fortunately, he seemed entirely distracted by something outside and behind him. He lifted his rifle and let off a long burst as a copter soared by.

Dash gasped as she recognized the pilot. "Toni!" she exclaimed, then put her hand over her mouth in dismay, watching the man just outside on the open deck. He had surely heard her.

But the glass was thick, and the copter noise, loud enough to be heard even inside, masked her shout. Alexei looked toward the bow in frustration for a moment, then turned and ran back the way he'd come.

Chance pulled Dash away from the window, back to the piano bar. She turned to Dash to ask about strategy. "Do we go after Dmitri, Alexei, or Toni?" she asked.

Dash frowned in concentration for a moment. "Dmitri is still the right person," she concluded. "If we have him, he can take care of everyone else." They turned toward the staircase.

And the deck slid out from under their feet as the ship heeled over.

Alexei watched forlornly as the copter disappeared around the bulkhead in front of him, flying toward the bow.

He hated this damn boat. Staircases everywhere, none

of them in the right place or going to the right level. He was on the outer edge of the second deck and there was no way to go forward, or even into the ship, except to go back to the stern and come back through the salon from there. Bah! So back he ran, figuring he could at least grab Vasily or Gleb and get them involved in some real work rather than just hanging out with the pretty girls.

Alexei just hated the way Dmitri treated him and his partner like unkempt half-wolves. Sure, he'd been known to have a little rough sex from time to time, but the rape charges had always been thrown out. He knew perfectly well how to behave with ladies.

But when he ran into the salon, he found that there were no ladies there, either figuratively or literally. He stopped dead for a second, then spotted the tied-up and blindfolded bodies of his comrades. He started to roar in rage, then swallowed it. No sense giving away his location to anyone listening.

What had the little girls done, anyway? While he'd never thought Gleb and Yefim were in his class, he'd always thought they were reasonably competent. From the bruises on their heads, he thought they might have been hit with baseball bats. Odd—there were no bats on board.

A little care seemed in order. He forced himself to reassess the girls as combatants.

If he ran into them he'd take them, but for the moment the copter was the threat. He had to get to the upper decks. Sigh. He'd have to go through the piano bar and up the staircase through Dmitri's suite, hopefully avoiding a demand for a full report on things he didn't know yet. He accelerated across the salon, then the ship slid sideways, throwing him into the frame of the entrance to the bar.

He just hated this damn boat.

Dmitri was sitting in the forward cabin of his main suite looking out over the sea at the gaggle of ships heading his way and talking on his radio when he heard the first gunfire towards the stern. The voice on the radio spoke. "What was that sound in the background?"

Dmitri closed his eyes. "Gunfire. You should get here as fast as possible."

"Of course. We are coming at full speed." Dmitri could see the Russian cruiser plowing the sea as it came toward him. His own *Buccaneer* also moved as fast as she could, which was a measly fifteen knots.

Dmitri sat for a few moments wondering what if anything he should do. Deciding to comm his captain to see what all his instruments said, he started to call up the bridge when another burst of gunfire arose, now on the port side. A brilliant silver copter—probably Matt's new baby; he'd heard about it and was thinking about getting one himself—banked in to touch down on the roof of the deck below him, which was to say, right in front of him just outside the window. He saw Toni jump out as the copter lifted off again. Both Toni and copter moved to starboard.

Instead of calling his captain, Dmitri spoke again to the cruiser captain. "Things are getting complicated here. Please send your helicopter."

"We should have done that in the first place," the cruiser captain grumbled.

Dmitri grunted.

Dmitri had always joked that all great Russian literature could be summed up as two rats dying in a gutter discussing philosophy. He looked thoughtfully at his wine glass with the gold-enameled lip. At least he wasn't in a gutter.

He heard gunfire overhead, from the bridge, and saw fragments of glass fall onto the roof deck in front of him where the copter had landed. He was not as surprised as he could have been when the Buccaneer banked into a turn in violation of his orders.

As the yacht heeled over, Dash and Chance instinctively grabbed the edge of the lustrous mahogany bar in front of a display of bottles of elegant alcoholic beverages. Fortunately, the bottles were snugly set, so although the liquid sloshed, nothing came flying to hit them. Apparently, the piano across the room was dogged to the deck. It stayed firmly planted as the pull of gravity shifted beneath them.

A soft yelp and a thump caused them to turn and see Alexei, who was not firmly planted at all unless you considered that his face was planted against the doorframe.

Chance saw her opportunity. She half-jumped, half-fell against him, pinning the AK-47 between them. She rotated her upper body and swung with her fist from the hips. It was not an ideal punch, but the sound of Alexei's head bouncing off the doorframe while his cheekbones crunched was satisfactory.

Damn, she'd hurt her hand. Careless. She wouldn't be assisting Dash with surgeries anytime soon, except maybe her own.

Still, she had to take advantage of the momentum while she had it. Alexei weighed about twice as much as she did, was probably even stronger, and had the damn gun besides. She twisted into an elbow strike just beneath his ear. This yielded another satisfying double-bang as his head slammed into the doorframe again.

Alexei sagged. The shifting of the boat now pulled her away from him. She prepared to kick but saw it was unnecessary. Pausing only to snatch up the gun, she shouted, "Dmitri!"

The staircase was right there, and she and Dash ran up it.

Dash was in the lead, figuring people were less likely to shoot her since she was the one they wanted to kidnap. She heard a click behind her and the snapping of the bolt in a gun, followed by a clank as the magazine hit the floor two decks below them. The bullet from the chamber rolled on a step behind her. She heard Chance mutter, "Guns. I have no idea what to do with them. Best to just make sure it can't hurt anybody."

They reached the next deck, which Dash guessed was Dmitri's private suite, just in time to see a man who must be the captain coming down another staircase, followed by a glaring Toni. Moments later Dmitri came through the passage from the bow. Toni pushed the captain aside and took careful aim at the yacht's owner.

Dmitri pulled up short. After a moment of assessment, he blinked and proceeded to speak with calm dignity. "Well. Looks like it's time for us to have another chat." He pointed back up the way Toni and the captain had come. "There's a nice conference room just in back of the bridge. Shall we move there?"

The ship was on robopilot, and the views from all the vidcams, radar, and sonar, were up on the wallscreen as everyone sat around the Round Table. They watched the little California Coastal Patrol hydrofoil successfully take the lead from the Russian cruiser. It did no good; they could see the helicopter approaching them at a speed no ship could rival.

Dash cleared her throat and spoke more calmly than she felt. "I say once again, they are only after me. Let me take the little boat on the stern deck and go to them. They'll leave you alone then."

Toni leaped up in rage. "Over my dead body!"

Dmitri shook his head. "They would like it that way. We need another plan. Ideally, one that allows me to survive as well." He looked mournful. "Though that seems most unlikely."

They saw Ted fly across the stern, blocking the view of the Russian helicopter for a moment. "Ah, I have it." He explained the plan. Toni called Ted, and everyone piled out of the conference room onto the copter platform.

Ted curved in and landed, carefully avoiding Vasily, who was curled in a corner of the pad. Dash ran toward the copter, saw Vasily, and paused to point at him. "Is he OK?" she demanded.

Toni looked uncomfortable. "More or less. I kind of poked out one of his eyes. And knocked him out."

Dash glared. "I thought you said you didn't do Krav Maga?"

Toni shrugged. "I said I did aikido better. I said I didn't *like* Krav Maga. I didn't say I couldn't do it. And if you're up against a guy who's standing there with a gun in his hand, it's quicker."

Dash had a dark suspicion. "Just how good are you at aikido, anyway?"

Toni shrugged. "Last time I competed, third best in Israel. But that was a while ago," she hastily qualified.

Dash shook her head. She started toward Vasily, hesitated, and stopped. No time. She pointed at Chance. "See what you can do to help him." She pointed at Dmitri. "And you! Your emergency medical equipment is abysmal. We will speak about it later."

She boarded the copter, and Ted took off again. As they soared around the ship and off toward the BrainTrust, Dmitri took a deep breath. "Now we'll see how many hours I have left." They all went back inside, and Dmitri called the Russian cruiser. "It's too late. The doctor got away on the copter that just left. Stand down."

The Russian cruiser captain cursed. "Pilot! See that silver copter? You heard what Mikhailov just said. Shoot it down, but do not hurt the doctor!"

"Captain, I... Are you sure?"

The captain growled.

"Aye, Captain."

Chance and the others watched as the Russian whirled past them. Chance waved at the pilot, then gave him the finger. "Matt's copter is faster. No way the Russians can catch up."

Dmitri answered gloomily, "It's not over till it's over."

Dash heard a *ping* from somewhere in the tail.

Ted exclaimed, "They're shooting at us!" He looked at his instruments. "Hang on." The little copter started to jink once more. "You OK there?"

Dash was hanging on for dear life to the seatbelt straps that crossed her chest. They didn't hold her in place any better when she clung to them, but it made her feel better. She was definitely developing serious motion sickness. She swallowed. "I am fine," she asserted gamely.

"Wow. This is some hardcore laser tag," Ted chirped. He was clearly not taking the whole situation seriously enough, but Dash did not think that pointing this out would improve his performance. She held on.

In a few moments, Ted whooped. "Just about to the reef. And we have backup!" Boats, copters, and drones were all speeding toward them. A couple of the copters had landed on the reef. "We're in the clear now."

There was another *ping,* and their copter started to spin. Ted grunted. "Hold on!" The spinning slowed as he regained control, but they were losing altitude fast—and they hadn't had much altitude to begin with. "Get ready to jump!" Ted shouted, more excited than afraid.

The copter hit the water rather gently, then settled. As

he popped the canopy, Ted said gleefully. "I designed it to float. Never got to check it out, though. Looks like my design was good."

Dash escaped from her seatbelt, then from the copter, into water that shocked her whole system with cold. The remains of her sarong were wrapped around her legs like Saran wrap, so she untied it and kicked it away. It was ironic, she thought, that she was wearing a bathing suit. It was as if she'd planned to spend her afternoon swimming away from a gunship. She focused on paying no attention to the violent shivering trying to take control of her limbs.

Dash was not a great swimmer, but she had dutifully taken the introductory swimming courses on the Brain-Trust, since, as Colin had said, *"You're living on a boat. Yes, it's a big, safe boat, but it's a big, dangerous ocean too. Knowing how to swim is just common sense."* After checking to make sure Ted was OK—no problem there, he swam like a fish—she side-stroked toward the reef, silently cursing her glasses, now coated in frothing seawater.

The copter flipped on its side suddenly and sank. Ted sighed. "Well, it almost worked."

Between gulps of air, and unintentional gulps of salt water as the waves came and went erratically, Dash offered comforting words. "It worked more than well enough, Ted. Thank you for rescuing me."

They heard the drone of the helicopter as they reached the reef. Ted replied, "We may not be out of the drink yet."

Two peacekeepers walked to the edge of the reef and offered assistance. One was a seeming giant, as pale as Ted. The other was just as tall but thinner, and about as dark as Dash. Both wore standard peacekeeper uniforms. Enough ocean spray had hit them to leech the shirts of their crispness, but the men still looked very determined and very professional. They pulled Dash and Ted from the water.

Dash stood up, shuddering once before regaining control. "Thank you."

The pale giant answered first. "Delighted to be of help, ma'am." He half-bowed. "Wolf Griffin at your service."

She looked him over carefully. His blond hair was cropped much closer than most she had seen. "So which military service gave you your training?" she asked, knowing it would be a terrible mistake to guess wrong.

"Marines, ma'am. Semper Fi."

Dash nodded. "Ever faithful. I'm surprised to see you on the BrainTrust. Is that not disloyal to your home country?"

Wolf pursed his lips. "In my day, we took an oath to the United States. Nowadays the kids take an oath to the President for Life. My Daddy always used to say, 'Loyalty above all things, son. Except for honor.'"

Dash nodded. "Well said, and wisely." She turned to the other man, who wore a turban. The turban was folded with a distinctive inverted "V" above the forehead. "You're a Sikh?"

The man stood straighter. "Most people think I'm a Muslim." He smiled appreciatively at her. "But then everyone says you're not most people."

Wolf roared with laughter and slapped the Sikh on the shoulder. "That's for sure." He looked at Dash and nodded toward the other man. "Aar here is a Khalsa. An elite warrior."

Aar rolled his eyes. "Not anymore."

Wolf shook his head. "OK, he's a lapsed Khalsa."

Dash studied Aar carefully, then realized the problem. "You trimmed your beard."

Aar nodded. "Unforgivable."

The droning of the helicopter grew louder, and Wolf stepped in front of Dash. "Stay behind me, ma'am."

Dash hopped out in front of him and, standing as tall as she could, threw her arms wide. "No, get behind me, both of you. They are under strict orders not to harm me. I will protect you."

Aar gurgled in helpless laughter. "Protected by an itty bitty girl. Captain, you're never going to live this down."

Dash found herself thinking about what a sight they made. Here she was, in an immodest bathing suit protecting a hulking Marine with her body, facing one of the most powerful assault copters ever built.

How had she wound up here, anyway? Had she made such poor decisions in this life? Could it be punishment for some transgression in a previous life? And above all, how long would it take for this absurd incident to be forgotten?

Then she noticed that the copters and boats that had been coming to her rescue had all stopped behind the reef. Apparently, everyone was confident that her two peace-keepers could defeat the Russian assault helicopter. This comforted her until she realized that half of the people in those copters were now taking videos, no doubt already going viral. This absurd moment would never be forgotten. Her parents would be apoplectic. Sigh.

Wolf snorted at Aar's earlier disparagement of his location behind Dash. "I'm not exactly happy about letting her stand there, but I'm not clear on how I'm supposed to stop her. And no one will question my masculinity, not to my face, anyway. And get yourself over here like the itty bitty girl told you to."

Dash heard a series of clanking sounds behind her. Moments later Wolf poked a long tube out over her shoulder, pointing at the copter. Dash recognized it with surprise. "Is that Ping's Big Gun?"

Wolf chortled. "Just like it. Ping was sooo looking forward to being the first person to use one in live combat. I am sooo looking forward to beating her to the punch, then sending her a detailed report on its operational effectiveness."

Dash heard a rising whine as the gun prepared to fire. The helicopter roared closer. Wolf hummed with delight.

Then the helicopter twisted sideways and veered away.

"Damn— I mean, gosh darn." The captain sighed. "I guess I don't get to be first."

Aar watched the copter shrink in the distance. "We always suspected the Russians had good intel. They must know about Ping's Big Gun. Otherwise, they'd have kept on coming."

The Big Gun lifted up and away, and Dash put her arms down. For a moment there was quiet.

Dash started to mutter thanks to the two men. Then she remembered what Ping had been trying to teach her for several weeks, trying to make her more American. It was time, she realized, to make Ping proud, no matter how shocking and unBalinese it was. She turned and put her arms around Wolf in a quick hug. "Thank you," she said, then turned and hugged Aar, "for saving my life."

Aar cleared his throat in surprise. "Just one of the services we offer, ma'am."

The sound of a different growling engine rose, and a sea-green speedboat with the words Stray Cat on its side charged toward them.

Wolf nodded at the boat. "I think that's our ride, ma'am."

A gleaming navy-blue copter separated from the pack overhead. Dash could see Gina's flaming red hair in the pilot's seat. Dash pointed at her. "Actually, Wolf, I think that is *my* ride." She beamed at the two men. "Thank you again. I'll tell Ping how helpful you both have been. And I will convey your disappointment at not getting to use the Big Gun first."

Wolf prodded Aar. *"Joe Bolay So Nihal."*

"Sat Sri Akal!" Aar offered what was obviously a Sikh battle cry.

"Oorah!" Wolf assented.

7

COMPLEX ALLIES

Nothing is certain but death and taxes.
—Benjamin Franklin

We have people working on both of those.
—Mark Miller, Chief Architect, Xanadu

The Chief Advisor listened with minimal patience to his good friend, the Russian Union Premier.

The Premier reiterated his assurance. "Dmitri Mikhailov was acting entirely on his own. I haven't confirmed this yet, but he was probably acting in conjunction with the Russian mob. I'm afraid the secret is pretty much out now that Dr. Dash has a rejuvenation process. Everybody wants it. Honestly, once you get your hands on it, I'd appreciate a chance to use it myself."

The Advisor relaxed. "And I promise, once I've got it, you're at the top of my list of friends to share it with."

"Thank you. Meanwhile, I assure you that Dmitri will

be punished appropriately for his grievous error. Very appropriately."

The Advisor shuddered. He knew what the Premier considered to be an appropriate punishment for just about everything that pissed him off. "Whatever. Till another day." They hung up.

Well, he'd been pretty sure that the Premier hadn't been behind the kidnapping despite the evidence. He was glad to have that confirmed.

But that still left him with a serious problem. After the failure of his Seal team to acquire the doctor some months ago, he'd been left without a viable backup plan. The time had come for more desperate measures…before somebody like the Russian mob got her. He felt a moment of panic. He had to get the President for Life rejuvenated. He was running out of time.

Dash sat down heavily in one of the chairs at the small table in her office. As she willed her body not to tremble, she reached out to cup the jade figurine of Ganesha, the God of Wisdom and remover of obstacles, in her hands. Even Ganesha, however, could not prevent the deaths of her patients.

Chance rushed into the room and took the chair opposite her. "You didn't have to tell the families alone," she said. "Shucks, you didn't have to tell them at all. You could've left the families to me."

Dash shook her head. "It is my therapy that is killing them, it is my responsibility to watch over them, and ultimately, it is my duty to tell their families." She sighed. "It is hard, but we must look on the bright side. The results this time were better than the first round."

Chance nodded. "I've read the reports. In your first tests, your patients were twice as likely to die as they were to rejuvenate. This time, we had four deaths, two patients who experienced no effect, and four successful rejuvenations for ten to fifteen years apiece. You've basically doubled the successful rejuvenation rate."

"It is still entirely unsatisfactory. It must be improved upon." Dash pulled out her tablet. After syncing the tablet to the wallscreen, she pulled up a list of ten new patient candidates. "This is our next group. They have all been vetted by Dark Alpha 42."

Chance blinked at the list. "'Dark Alpha 42?' What on earth is that?"

"It is one of the startup companies on the *Dreams Come True*. They have an AI by the same name they have been developing. It is a far-reaching enhancement of the Alpha Zero AI."

Chance rolled her eyes. "OK, and what's the Alpha Zero?"

"It was an AI that shook the research world way back in 2017. After just four hours of training, it was one of the best chess-playing programs in the world."

Chance eyed the list of patients. "Cool! So what's the AI's explanation for what makes these patients more suitable for the current version of the therapy?"

"I have no idea," Dash responded. "The Dark Alpha series of AIs don't offer explanations. Like the original Alpha Zero, which integrated two very human systems of

AI with a nonhuman neural network learning algorithm, the Dark Alphas all have nonhuman elements. Dark Alpha 42 has the most nonhuman elements of any AI ever built, and the least chance of explaining anything in a way that a person could understand."

A look of alarm overcame Chance's features. "But… that's illegal! All AIs are required to give simple explanations for all their decisions. Any analysis that uses insights beyond human understanding must be discarded."

Dash tilted her head from side to side indecisively. "Well, that is not entirely true. It is true that the European Union, back in 2017, passed regulations that would bankrupt companies that used AI-driven decisions that could not be easily explained. At first, enforcement was weak, and companies could get away with simply putting yet another checkbox in front of the user to authorize the AI. But as enforcement grew more stringent over the course of the next decade, research into nonhuman analysis processes withered and died."

By this time, Chance had figured out where the discussion was going. "Of course! Except it didn't really die, did it? It only died dirtside. Nonhuman AI survived—and continued to evolve—here on the BrainTrust. Right? And while it would be wonderful to have a nice simple explanation from a more human AI that we could use to separate good rejuvenation candidates from those who would die, we are much better off with good decisions with no explanations than we were with poor decisions with good explanations."

Dash smiled brightly. "Welcome to your first BrainTrust moment. That moment when you realize that things that are not possible elsewhere happen every day here. Do not worry. I still have BrainTrust moments like that myself." She headed out the door. "Shall we go break some laws and save some lives?"

Mediator Joshua Pickett softly sang *Goodbye, Columbus* as he walked from his home on the *Chiron* over to the *Haven*. Most people would've taken an arvee between the ships, but he considered that silly since it really wasn't all that far away. The total distance from his home to his office was less than a kilometer; little more than a ten-minute walk, too short to even make using a bicycle worthwhile, much less a car.

Besides, he enjoyed the view as he walked across the gangways that connected the isle ships. The plexiglass tunnel connecting the *Chiron* to the *Elysian Fields* showed a particularly impressive sight, the iridescent superstructure of the *Elysian Fields*, across which flowed a brilliant display of swirling colors much like the titanium jewelry it had been stressed to mimic.

Another advantage to walking was the opportunity to stop at Joy's Coffee Hut on the promenade of the *Dreams Come True* before crossing the last gangway onto the *Haven*. He was sitting there stirring two packets of sugar into his caramel frappuccino when Mediator Chibuzo walked up to him, chuckling. "So, Joshua, I hear you can run from trouble, but trouble will find you nonetheless."

Joshua looked up from his tablet. "Darnell, nice to see you, but I have no idea what you're talking about."

Darnell took the seat across from him and gave him a guttural laugh. "So you haven't seen your docket for today yet? And you haven't read the news?" He slapped a beefy hand on the table. "Man, you have all the luck, and you don't even know it yet!"

Joshua, who had been bringing his coffee up to his lips, carefully put the coffee down. He now had a very bad feeling.

Just recently, Joshua had asked Mediator Chibuzo to take his place on the *Chiron*. Joshua's specialty was mediating contract disputes. His recent cases, however, had all been outside the realm of his expertise. A peacekeeper dressed like a hooker had been assaulted by an attempted client. An honor killing gone wrong, since the woman to be killed was an ex-Pakistani commando. An eco-terrorist who had blown up one of the *Chiron's* nuclear reactors in hopes of laying waste to the archipelago. Exciting and interesting to be sure, but enough was enough. He'd figured Darnell might enjoy the change of pace if this sort of thing continued.

Meanwhile, the arrival of the *Haven*, filled with billionaires starting up new ventures all over the BrainTrust, had seemed like a gift from heaven. He'd applied to be their mediator and had immediately been accepted, presumably because they'd looked at his credentials and thought he made an excellent match.

In practice, he'd mediated more divorces than business disputes in the weeks since the *Haven* had arrived, but he'd nonetheless had a very satisfactory run of cases. Simple for a man of his background, and quiet. He'd rather enjoyed the quiet.

Darnell interrupted this reverie. "I'm just going to sit here until you read the local GNews headlines." He folded his hands with the clear intent of waiting, however long it took. "Someone needs to be able to report your expression when you see what's happening."

Sighing, Joshua pulled out his tablet and punched up the headlines. The top story screamed at him: Russian Oligarch Attempts to Kidnap Our Dr. Dash.

Joshua read no further. The rest was obvious. The Americans had tried to kidnap Dash once before, and now the Russians had taken a shot. And of course, the oligarch who ran the operation was necessarily a resident of the *Haven*. And of course, to further simplify the matter, the kidnapping had surely been attempted while on the *Haven*. Therefore, it was Joshua's case to mediate.

Joshua put his hands over his eyes and groaned. "This can't be real," he muttered. He repeated this new mantra three times before opening his eyes again.

Mediator Chibuzo watched him gleefully. "Oh, that was everything I could've hoped for." He rose, and offered as he departed, "I have to go tell everybody how satisfying it was watching you learn the news."

Joshua had visions of Darnell talking with all the other mediators on the BrainTrust. He groaned again.

The Chief Advisor frowned down at the President for Life as he did every month at this time. The President lay on the hospital bed wired like a Christmas tree as an armada of computers monitored his medically-induced coma.

Maintaining him in this state, the doctors had explained years ago, slowed the rate of his decay. Not to worry about problems from the early days of induced-coma tech, they said. Electrostim kept the muscles in top shape, and chemically-induced stimulation did the same for the rest of the organs.

The fact that keeping him comatose prevented him from issuing constant demands was just a side benefit.

A handful of doctors and nurses crowded around, modifying the drips and sensors, bringing the President slowly back to awareness. Too slowly. The Advisor turned to the doctor in charge. "We don't have time for this. I'm calling in the professionals."

The doctor looked at him glumly. "We can handle this."

"Too late." The Advisor went to the door and called, "Ladies, you're up."

Two porn stars and a centerfold swished into the room. They stripped down to their work clothes and went to work on the President.

The Chief Advisor, unable to watch them perform for more than a moment, turned away from the sight.

The doctor joined him. "I just hate that this works so well."

The Chief Advisor shrugged. "Don't take it personally. They're very good at their business. Trixie hand-picked them herself." And sent them to him for a final in-depth interview before giving them the job. Really, had any national leader ever had an admin as wonderful as Trixie?

A low animal sound rose behind them, amidst the sounds of gentle female laughter. The Advisor shuddered, knowing he'd never be able to get those sounds out of his head. Still, he had to try. He drifted into philosophical rumination as he often did at this point. It was fascinating to consider the gradual steps that had led them here.

In retrospect, the first symptom of the President's geriatric trouble had been mental. He'd come up with increasingly outrageous conspiracy theories and invented ever more wildly ridiculous facts on the fly. No one realized it was a problem, however, since this was indistinguishable from his usual behavior.

But after his physical condition had started deteriorating as well, his beliefs became so bizarre even BreitTart no longer defended them. That was when the guy carrying the nuclear football quietly took the gold card from the President and handed it to the Chief Advisor.

Misty's six-inch heels clicked as she came around to confront him, still wearing her work clothes. The Chief Advisor carefully kept his eyes focused on her face. He'd learned long ago that if he let his eyes wander, he could no longer understand what she was saying.

She jutted out a hip and put her hand on it. "He's up." She looked past him and smiled mischievously. "In more ways than one." A pause. "Ok, now he's actually standing up. And going down." Another wicked gleam entered her eyes. "Oh, wait, that's what I'll be doing later."

The Chief Advisor put his hand up to rub his temples. In another ironic twist, he suspected Misty enjoyed her job more than the Chief Advisor enjoyed his. "Let's get this show on the road."

As the ladies got dressed, the President leaned over his walker and followed his guides out to the podium. They set up the framework that would invisibly hold him upright as he spoke. The Chief Advisor grabbed his teleprompter remote control and headed to his usual location, off to the side of the stage but still visible to the President from the corner of his eye.

Once they had the President positioned and locked in, they opened the doors to let in the reporters. They came to hear the speech, of course, but more importantly, they came to see that the President was still alive and going strong.

The President began speaking, with remarkable vitality for someone so deathly weakened by age and the acute attention deficit disorder that had plagued him even before he became President.

The Chief Advisor listened to the speech with only half an ear. He had stopped paying attention to the main body of the speech years ago, just making sure there were enough superlatives: "Greatest in history," "Most magnificent ever," "Absolutely wonderful," and so on.

They came to the critical part of the speech, the part where the President would go off-script. The President's followers always went wild for this part. The off-script section was the key to letting everyone know that the President was still their man; that he had not yet bowed to the forces of the deep state. Since the off-script part was so important, it was the most carefully scripted part of the whole presentation.

For a moment near the end of the off-script segment, the President hesitated. It looked for a second like he would go off the off-script. The Chief Advisor raised his remote control and pressed the button.

The teleprompter had been customized just for the

President. In addition to the words rolling by, the display showed an image of the people who would be entertaining the President after the speech concluded. Normally, it showed the three ladies.

When the Chief Advisor pressed the button, the image changed. The new image that came into sharp focus reminded the President that if he behaved badly, he would not be entertained by the ladies, but rather by Darren.

The President's eyes bulged. After another hesitation, he returned to the main script.

A short while later it was over. The Chief Advisor exhaled slowly. The ladies would now entertain the President till he was exhausted and nearly comatose. The doctor would take it from there.

Someday, the doctor would wind up declaring the President clinically deceased. The Chief Advisor planned to call in the ladies and give them a last shot. He would see if they could actually raise the dead. He figured they had one chance in three.

Another monthly speech had gone off without a hitch, but the whole process reminded the Advisor that such a smooth operation could not run forever. The President needed rejuvenation, dammit! If the bastard had the gracelessness to die the country would explode, the same way that Kestrel rocket had exploded so recently.

Now the Kestrels were out on the damn BrainTrust with the damn doctor who held the damn secret to fixing the damn President. He had to grab the doctor. Just sending the Seals hadn't been enough. To succeed, the Seals would need a really good diversion the next time; something bigger and better than an idiotic eco-terrorist with a dinky backpack bomb.

And then he understood what to do, and how to do it. He almost melted into his chair with relief when he got back to his office. He'd have Trixie bring in some champagne so the two of them could celebrate. Maybe he'd even celebrate with his wife later as well. Of course, he couldn't really tell either of the women what they were celebrating, namely—

The gigantic diversion he needed could be easily arranged.

Joshua watched in glum amazement as the participants in the latest fracas filed into his room. He started by examining the victims. As he had come to expect in these cases, the victims looked mostly unharmed. As he had also come to expect, the assailants looked thoroughly beaten and battered. He turned his attention to the young woman wearing a white lab coat. "Dash. It's good to see you again, but perhaps we should arrange to meet under other circumstances in the future."

Dash gave him a sunny smile. "It is my pleasure to see you, Mediator Joshua. I was so happy when I heard that you would once again take charge of the proceedings."

Joshua kept a smile fixed on his face as he turned to the next woman facing him. "Amanda. Let me guess. The Chairman of the Board for the BrainTrust Consortium considers this case sufficiently important to the archipelago as a whole that she felt obligated to take time from her busy schedule to act once more as a friend of the mediation."

Amanda smiled as warmly as Dash had a moment earlier. "There are...complications here. Colin thought I might help."

Joshua struggled to maintain his fixed smile. "'Complications.'" If *Amanda* thought there were complications, he was in deep trouble. And if Colin thought there were complications...but then, he'd suspected that already. *This can't be real*, he reminded himself, but he found himself unconvincing.

Next, he turned to the tall young woman standing next to Dash. "Ms. Dixon, I presume?"

Dash interrupted, "Doctor Dixon would be more appropriate."

Ms./Dr. Dixon stared at Dash. "Well, not quite yet."

Dash gave her a big grin. "I've been waiting for the right opportunity to tell you. Today seems like a good day."

Dr. Dixon looked dazed, then she too smiled brightly. "Dr. Dixon. It does sound good, doesn't it?" She looked back at Joshua. "Regardless, please call me Chance. Dash has been telling me great stories about you. Nice to meet you, Your Honor."

He was facing too many bright smiles not to feel warmed, so he smiled back. "I'm not a judge, Dr. Dixon. Chance. Call me Mediator Joshua during the proceedings, please."

He turned to the next woman facing him. "And you must be Toni Shatzki, the Good Samaritan."

Toni grimaced. "Well, I helped Dash out as best I could. Of course, Ted actually got her off the ship."

Having read all the accounts of the kidnapping by all the participants, Joshua glanced at the assailants. One of them sported a thick pad where he had once had an eyeball. A result, he remembered, of Toni's rather vigorous effort to help Dash as best she could. Joshua responded in a dry tone, "Dash always seems to have remarkably helpful friends. I confess I had a few qualms when Ping and Jam left. I guess I'm pleased to have my fears allayed. I guess." He raised an eyebrow at Amanda.

Amanda nodded. "Colin."

"Of course." Next, he turned to the alleged assailants. He frowned. "Dmitri Mikhailov. I'm astonished to find you here. When I first arrived, I confess I expected to find you at the heart of an endless stream of vicious contract disputes. When that didn't happen, I was delighted. Yet now here you are, in the center of a dispute much more distasteful than anything in contract law. What do you have to say in your defense?"

"First, Your Honor, I wanted to make it clear that I undertook this kidnapping attempt on my own, and the Premier of the Russian Union had nothing to do with it." Dmitri stared straight ahead, not even raising his hand to wipe the sweat from his brow.

Once again Joshua had to freeze the expression on his face to avoid displaying his astonishment. He'd heard people confess before, but none so carefully articulate in protecting another person who wasn't even a part of the dispute. He suspected he'd just heard the beginning of Amanda's complications. "I, ah, will take that into account in my final determinations." He wasn't exactly sure how he would take it into account, but he'd burn that bridge when he came to it. One more question before moving on to the next assailant. "There's no mention in any of the accounts of this incident of you getting physically harmed. You look fine. Do you have any injuries to declare?"

As usual, when a matter of medical status came up, Dash spoke first. "He is unharmed." She pursed her lips. "Unjust as that may be."

Ms. Dixon/Dr. Dixon/Chance chirped up, "As soon as Toni pointed the gun at him, he folded. After that, he was the perfect gentleman."

Joshua looked at Toni. Toni shrugged. "I actually think he was driven as much by his own sense of guilt as he was by the gun." She nodded slowly. "Though I think the gun would have been fully persuasive all on its own."

Joshua looked at the other four assailants. They all looked a little like zombies to him. He looked at the sheet of names. "Gleb, Vasily, Alexei, Yefim, you all look barely able to stand. Should I send you all back to the med bay and hold this mediation later?"

Dash explained, "They all experienced significant head trauma. Concussions." She paused. "It is best for them to stay awake at this time. Standing here is good for them." Joshua wondered if he heard just a hint of satisfaction in her voice.

Yefim started to topple over, and a peacekeeper behind him lifted him back to his feet.

Joshua frowned at Dash, but then Chance jumped in. "I concur with the doctor's advice." She beamed. "I'm qualified to offer a diagnosis as well now."

Vasily slumped, and another peacekeeper held him up.

Joshua looked at the third doctor in the room, Amanda.

Amanda stood serenely, like a Madonna, radiating calm certainty. "I have not examined the patients myself, but the assessment seems reasonable. I have complete confidence in my doctors."

Joshua scanned the three of them, all presenting a united front, not a hint of weakness or doubt. For a moment, he could have sworn he saw of the ghost of Hippocrates rise up behind them, shrug his shoulders, and mouth the words, "Just Go With It." Joshua blinked the hallucination away. He had no choice but to take the advice, anyway.

Joshua focused on Vasily. And on his eye patch. "And the eye?"

Dash spoke with clear regret this time. "He'll need a new electronic eye. It can never be as good, and it will be quite expensive."

Amanda said heatedly, "An expense we are under no obligation to undertake."

Dmitri looked at Joshua. "I will pay for the eye. It's the least I can do."

Joshua told Dmitri grimly, "It's only the beginning of what you're going to do. I presume none of your four accomplices have any money to compensate the victims? It's all coming out of your pocket."

Dmitri nodded in understanding. "Like I said, this is entirely my fault. The Premier had nothing to do with it. I was planning to sell Dash to the Russian mafia."

Again with the forceful clarification of the Premier's noninvolvement. Reflecting on the written accounts, Joshua noticed a particularly problematic issue with Dmitri's claim. "And yet you happened to have the captain of a Russian Navy cruiser—" Joshua bit off the rest of the sentence as he caught Amanda glaring at him. *Complications*, he reminded himself.

Something about his expression must have caught Dmitri's attention. "Mediator Joshua? Could I, ah, speak to you in private for a moment?"

Joshua closed his eyes. Complications. He motioned to Dmitri to come into his private chamber. Dmitri hesitated, but then followed him in and Joshua closed the door.

Joshua raised an eyebrow at him. "Well?"

"I am hoping you will allow Dash to come in and speak with us as well. It's a matter of life and death, actually." He grimaced. "I doubt I'll have another opportunity to speak to her after these proceedings are over. I doubt anyone will let me near her after this."

Joshua manfully refrained from offering his own biting assessment. Even if he didn't order it, he doubted anyone would let Dmitri on the same ship with her, much less within speaking distance. He'd be lucky to survive an attempt to talk to her with only a concussion.

Again Dmitri spoke sincerely. "But it really *is* a matter of life and death."

Joshua allowed the request to hang in the air for a moment. When he realized he was savoring Dmitri's anxiety—very unprofessional—he nudged himself into action. He opened the door again and waved. "Dash, I need you for a moment."

Dash looked at Dmitri with puzzled suspicion but came obediently into Joshua's chambers. She took a position on the far side of the room from her prior assailant. At least it would be entertaining to watch the oligarch try to wrangle a favor from the good doctor.

Dmitri knelt on the carpet, bringing himself to eye level with Dash. He spoke beseechingly. "I was wondering if you know anything about polonium poisoning."

The carefully controlled anger on Dash's face gave way to bafflement, then bemusement. "Polonium?"

With a blinding burst of insight, Joshua understood the situation. Against his better judgment, he found himself feeling sorry for Dmitri.

He realized in yet another painful flash of clarity that if he were a true professional, he would intervene on behalf of the poor billionaire. *The poor billionaire!* Once again the fickle gods of irony had snuck to Joshua's side to become his boon companions. "Dash," he said softly, "because Dmitri failed in his attempt to kidnap you, he expects the Premier to assassinate him."

Dmitri enlarged on Joshua's explanation. "His weapon of choice in cases like this is a touch of polonium." He pulled the stylus from his tablet and poked himself on the back of the hand. "A quick jab, a sharp tip with the merest hint of polonium, barely noticeable under the best of circumstances, and all that's left of your life is a slow painful death."

Dash's eyes widened, then narrowed. She pointed a finger at him accusingly. "You lied."

Befuddlement swept across Dmitri's face. Joshua sympathized. Dmitri had lied about so many things, which one stood out so strongly that Dash would get incensed about it in particular?

Her finger still pointed sternly at the culprit. "You

weren't really going to sell me to the Russian mafia. I knew it."

After a moment's astonishment, Dmitri bellowed a good Russian laugh. "Certainly not."

Dash turned to Joshua. "And you believe him? The Premier would really murder Dmitri like that?"

Joshua licked his lips. "It's the Premier's signature form of assassination. Using polonium, no one can prove he's behind it, but everyone knows he's responsible."

Dash nodded. "There just are not that many people with access to a ready supply of polonium." She stared back at Dmitri thoughtfully, her expression turning to anger once more as she thought about the Premier. And then her expression changed ever so slightly, and Joshua saw a darkly terrifying glint in Dash's eyes. He realized at that moment just how deadly a genius like her could be if she chose to be so.

Then her look of cold rage dissolved into one of horror. She put her hand over her mouth. Wide-eyed, she muttered, "Oh no. I just had a very bad thought."

And she was back again; the old, comforting Dash. Turning to Dmitri, she offered her analysis. "There is, to my knowledge, no cure for polonium poisoning. However, I believe some experiments have been conducted with chelating agents—chemicals that capture metal atoms. Of course, chelating agents tend to be highly toxic." She paused. "I'll see what I can come up with."

Dmitri bowed his head. "Thank you. Thank you."

After waving them from his chambers, Joshua took a few moments to think about his verdict before going back to the cast of characters in the mediation room. He could not, he realized, send Dmitri back to Russia as he normally would. Dash would not permit it, even if he were willing to do it. He tried to think of something novel for a proper punishment, above and beyond an extraordinary amount of victim compensation, but the necessary creative insight escaped him. With a sigh, he rejoined the others.

He'd thought that the final declaration of damages would be anti-climactic after the intensity of the sidebar, but in this he was not quite as correct as he'd expected. "Mr. Mikhailov, assuming you pay the compensation I am about to specify, you may stay on the BrainTrust. However, your associates must return to Russia." He looked at the one with only one eye. "As soon as they are fit to travel."

Dmitri looked at him mournfully. "It's fine to send Alexei and Vasily back to their master, but I beseech you to let me keep Gleb and Yefim. I promise you they won't cause any trouble."

Joshua suspected Dmitri was overconfident on this point, but with the Premier prepping polonium death for him, Joshua supposed Dmitri might reasonably want a couple of trusted bodyguards with him. "Very well. I put them under your supervision. If they so much as twitch a finger wrong, you're the one who'll be paying the damages."

Dmitri nodded.

Joshua looked down at his tablet. "Let's wrap up here with the compensation due to the victims, Dr. Dash and Dr. Dixon."

Dash raised her hand as if she were in a classroom. "Mediator Joshua?"

More complexity? And he was so close to finishing this session. He sighed. "Yes, Dash?"

"In addition to the financial compensation that I am sure you will adjudge wisely, I have another demand of Dmitri I hope you will enforce for me."

Ah! Could this be the innovative punishment he'd sought? "I would be delighted to consider your proposal."

Dash squared her shoulders. "I require that Dmitri refurbish the medical compartment on board his yacht to my specifications. Honestly, for a ship with gold-plated faucets, his facilities to deal with accidents, injuries, and infections are an embarrassment. They must be improved upon."

Well, not quite as punishing as he had hoped for, but Joshua was happy to enforce this request. "As you wish."

Joshua looked down at his tablet. "To wrap up, here are the sums to be paid to Dash and Chance in compensation for the egregious violation of their persons." He named an amount.

Chance leapt into the air with a whoop, then fell to the floor, laughing, "I'm rich! I'm rich!" She sucked in a lungful of air. "I can't wait to tell my mom!"

Dash looked down at Chance, still rolling on the floor. Granted, Joshua's compensation was generous, but it was hardly worth having a fit over. Then she thought about her former patients on Bali. Desperately poor, many of them, considering themselves lucky if they had a motor scooter to hoist all three children aboard to drive to the market.

Such a sight they made swerving down the winding roads! So dangerous, yet so happy.

She visualized them receiving such riches. She saw them, whole extended families, dazed, struck dumb by their good fortune. She put her hand to her mouth again, this time in embarrassment. "Oh, my." Living on the Brain-Trust had severely damaged her concept of what it meant to be wealthy.

8

HOW TO BUILD A ROCKET AT HOME

If people live a lot longer it will be disastrous for the environment, so people working on this must be really unethical.

—Casual comment overheard in Berkeley, spoken in the tone of self-evident truth

Dash juggled the last of four large boxes into the back of an arvee. As she straightened, she saw Chance approach. "Chance!" she cried. "You are just in time to come with me to celebrate!" Dash hopped into one of the front seats and patted the other. "Come on."

Chance, quite mystified by this eagerly excited version of her boss, climbed into the seat next to her. "What are we celebrating?"

Dash just laughed. "You will know in just a couple of minutes."

As the car surged over the gangway to the *Elysian Fields*, Chance tried to guess where they were going. "Are we going to Dmitri's? Surely we're not getting on his yacht again."

Even this reference to their too-recent kidnapping was unable to break Dash's mood. "Lords, no. We are not going that far. We have a party on the *Dreams Come True*."

"Cool! Who's throwing the party?"

Dash giggled. "We are."

Their little arvee rolled into the nearest elevator once they were on the *Dreams*, then rolled out onto a Battlestar-themed deck. Here and there they passed Cylon warriors, the clunky metal ones from the first TV series, and federation officers engaging them in various forms of combat. In one scene, a tall Cylon played chess with a captain, while in another place a pair of Cylons were clearly fleecing a number of lieutenants in a game of poker. The arvee stopped in front of a side corridor with a small black sign etched in gold that read, Dark Alpha Corporation.

Chance now had a pretty good idea what they were celebrating. "So how were the results with our new set of patients?"

Dash gave a little leap in the air as she got out of the arvee. "You take the two boxes on your side, I'll take the two boxes on mine." Grabbing her boxes, Dash scurried into Dark Alpha's offices.

When Chance entered, she saw the receptionist frown as Dash rushed past her, disregarding polite protocol. Dash shouted, "Everybody! We have cake! Strawberry cake, lemon cake, and angel food. And chocolate! Come and get it!"

Chance muttered apologetically to the receptionist,

"She just saved a lot of people's lives using your AI. Why don't you come have a piece of cake?"

The receptionist gave her a forgiving smile and offered brightly, "Well then, I guess I better find a knife and some paper plates."

Chance found Dash cutting slices of cake with a scalpel and she sighed. "I guess you can take the surgeon out of the hospital, but you can't take the hospital out of the surgeon."

Fortunately, the receptionist arrived in time with the plates, knives, and forks. As they started passing cake around, a short man with feverish eyes and a stubbled chin suggesting he had worked in the office all night entered the conference room. Everyone turned to look at him, and Chance surmised he was the boss. His eyes widened. "Dash. What are you doing here?"

Dash handed him a piece of chocolate cake. "Everyone's alive. I have ten patients. One of them is showing no effect from the therapy, and the other nine are all showing signs of rejuvenation. No one is going to die."

The boss pumped his fist in the air. "Yes!" He turned to the receptionist. "Emily, don't we have some champagne around here someplace?" With that, the celebration turned into an all-afternoon affair.

After all the champagne and most of the cake had been consumed and every person there had congratulated every other person in the room on the key role they had played in this victory, Chance and Dash took another arvee back to their lab. As the vehicle rolled along, Chance pulled out her tablet. "Time to pick more patients, so I guess I want to submit this next list to Dark Alpha 42?"

"Not necessary." Dash took the tablet from her. She read

through the medical records of all the fresh candidates and checked off acceptance boxes. By this time they had reached their lab, and Chance sat patiently in the arvee until Dash had selected ten.

Finally, Dash handed the tablet back and climbed out of the vehicle. "There you go. Those should be fine patients for our next run."

Chance stood stock still as she studied the list. "Are you telling me that you've figured out how the AI selects new patients?"

Dash's eyes gleamed with mischievous laughter. "When I saw Dark Alpha 42's level of confidence in its predictions, I pulled a random sample of a couple of thousand patients from all over the *Chiron* and had the AI assess them. I then took all those examples, along with our historical patients, and studied them for more hours than I can count. Finally, I pulled another hundred patients from the database, and confirmed that I made the same selections as Dark Alpha."

Chance laughed, then looked eagerly into Dash's eyes. "That's great! So now that you know, tell me. How do we distinguish the viable candidates from the ones who would die?"

Dash opened her mouth to answer, then closed it again. Finally, she confessed, "I still do not know. I know how to pick them myself, but I cannot really express it in words." She twitched her nose. "Very disturbing."

Chance just shook her head. "Dash, I think someone slipped some nonhuman algorithms into your genetic coding."

Dash pursed her lips as they continued walking. "Very unlikely. Very unlikely indeed."

One of the nice things about horseback riding was the opportunity to contemplate irritating problems without distraction, and without feeling the irritation. Green grass stretched out before the Premier for kilometers, with only the occasional tree acting as an accent to the smooth perfection. This was a part of one of the Premier's private ranches, maintained just for his amusement.

He zipped his leather jacket against the nip in the air and took Thunder out at a trot. Thunder, true to form, sidled just a bit to the right as they started across the plain, hoping to reach the tree near the barn with the low-hanging branch that would sweep the Premier from the saddle. The Premier let Thunder play his little game for a few moments before correcting him. Beyond the tree, the Premier let Thunder speed up as the Premier turned his mental energy to his current problem and concomitant opportunity.

Yesterday the problem that he had taken horseback riding had still been getting his hands on the rejuvenation therapy. He had reluctantly concluded that since Dmitri had blown the best chance, his next step was to sit back and wait, counting on the Chief Advisor to get the girl and share the cure with his friends. It was unsatisfying to be reduced to the role of spectator, but he admitted a certain relief at having made the decision.

Today's irritation still resided with the BrainTrust, but the target had changed. His next problem was SpaceR.

SpaceR had been annoying him for a long time now. Once upon a time, the Russian space program had been an enormously profitable undertaking. Nobody had rockets that could lift as much payload as the Russian Proton heavy lifter. She had been the queen of the skies.

Acting just like any good capitalist, the Premier had charged prices every bit as amazing as the size of the Proton's payloads, but then SpaceR had come out with the reusable Kestrel Heavy.

Disaster. How swiftly his loyal customers had betrayed him. How swiftly his mighty Proton had fallen. The only way he'd been able to keep the Russian rocket program alive was by launching all of Russia's own satellites with them, which was enormously expensive. The Russian rockets had cost a fortune, not only because of the profits he extracted but because of their underlying exorbitant costs.

Now the rocket business was looking up. The itty bitty computer bug he'd had planted in the chips on the Kestrel Heavy had finally caused one to explode.

It had been a careful dance.

When the American government had started debating yet again after yet another minor terrorist attack whether to force all computer chips from all manufacturers to have built-in backdoors, the Premier had been delighted. He had put all the Russian trolls and bots on all the social media to work supporting the proposal. The result had been every-thing he could have hoped for.

The American government had assured the people that no one would be able to use the back door except the always honorable and ever-incorruptible employees of the United States government, along with their contractors and their subcontractors. The crypto geeks had established a five-by-seven encryption system. Seven people had partial keys for the backdoor. Opening it required a subset of five of them to get together and combine their sub-keys.

It was a sweet system, mathematically elegant enough to make his own crypto geeks swoon. As a practical matter, it was also delightfully straightforward to break. Bribe one key holder, blackmail another one, infect the computer that belonged to a third with a quiet virus, and plant a miniature vidcam in the office of a fourth. The Premier's own crypto people had broken the fifth sub-key by exploiting a weakness in the random number generator used to create it.

The Premier could now use the back door more easily than could the president of the country that had created it in the first place. The President for Life and the Chief Advisor still had to bring five of the key holders together to break into the chips, whereas the Premier had gone the extra distance to combine all five sub-keys into a functioning super-key on his personal computer. As a consequence, the Chief Advisor tended to access the most confidential materials created by his enemies and his potential enemies only about once a week, whereas the Premier could do so on a daily basis.

While the Premier used his access religiously to eavesdrop and spy, he was very judicious indeed in using the backdoor to insert fake news, computer bugs, or viruses. It would be terrible if people became aware that he had full power over all the computers in the world. Everybody with real secrets would switch to using the BrainTrust chips in which the backdoor circuitry had been removed.

So when he had decided to cripple SpaceR to make the

Proton rocket once again a viable platform for commercial sales, he'd had his programmers create a virus that inserted just the tiniest statistical risk into the Kestrel Heavy's engine behavior. The virus introduced a barely meaningful delay into the responsiveness of the fuel valve controllers that had to ensure that all twenty-seven engines were creating exactly the same amount of thrust at exactly the same time. The Premier's programmers figured that about one time in a hundred the consequent fluctuation would shake and vibrate the boosters to the extent that something catastrophic would happen.

It had all worked just about as he had hoped.

Honestly, he would have preferred to have had the accident occur with a capsule full of people rather than a cargo of habitat cubes, but the death of the little girl's kitty had served very nearly as well. Perhaps even better. It looked for a while like the state of California would destroy SpaceR outright for him.

But not quite. The new CEO, Toscano, had pulled a fast one. Nicely done; the launch from the center of the Brain-Trust archipelago had been beautiful, he had to admit.

But every move led to a counter-move. California had taken a fabulously aggressive next step, and Toscano had responded in kind. Moving his whole manufacturing operation to the BrainTrust seemed like an act of desperation. Customers were noticing. People with cargoes so valuable they could afford a Proton were making inquiries already, just in case they needed a backup plan. A critical moment in the history of rocketry was upon them. Just a little push and the Premier would own the future.

So he'd go all out this time. No statistical vagaries here.

His man inside SpaceR would infect the new Kestrel Titan with a guaranteed set of rocket-killing viruses. The rocket would blow up seconds after leaving the pad. The whole Kestrel Titan line of boosters would be discredited and abandoned by paying customers.

Beautiful as SpaceR's first launch from the BrainTrust had been, this launch would supply the better spectacle. After all, everyone loved a good explosion.

Matt wore a pair of blue jeans, a polo shirt, loafers, and his battered old Tilley hat used for hiking in the Sierras. He boarded the ferry to San Diego. He looked like another scruffy tourist, exhausted from the continuous party on *Elysian Fields*. He did not think he would be arrested if the governor and the attorney general learned he was back in California, but he was not interested in finding out.

Meanwhile, Gina decked herself out with a white halter dress with matching purse and heels and took a copter back to San Francisco, where she hopped a plane to LAX, and grabbed a limo down to Palos Verdes. "Roberta!" she gushed as she rolled into her real estate agent's office. "New house time!"

Roberta looked puzzled, then smiled. "You've only been in your current house for what, a year? Is something wrong?"

"Very much so!" Gina exclaimed, throwing out a hip and putting her hand on it. "Matt's the CEO now. We need something bigger. Better for entertaining."

Roberta's smile got larger. "Yes, you certainly do. I'm so glad you're here."

And the two of them sat down together to work on the sale of the current home, while planning, once the sale was in place, the extended house-hunting expedition to find a suitable mansion as the replacement.

And Gina fully planned to go house-hunting, but only because she and Roberta always had a blast together. Alas, though Roberta would make a fine commission on the sale of the current house, she would be disappointed when the buying of another house fell through. Gina just hoped she could make it up to her someday, somehow.

But the BrainTrust was Gina's home now. Their house on the *Haven* might be cramped, but it was safe from the kind of civil forfeiture procedures already underway against SpaceR.

Civil forfeiture was much on the minds of other people as well. Tom Patterson, the boss of International Association of Machinists and Aerospace Workers Local 1953, stood menacingly in the governor's office. Heavy-set, he had a jovial smile that had become his signature in college after a close-up photo taken with a zoom lens caught it. He had smiled in that same way under his helmet after he'd tackled a wide receiver and knocked the football from the opponent's hands into the hands of a teammate. The teammate had then run it back for a touchdown.

His team had played Matt Toscano's Notre Dame once in a playoff. Tom liked to think that he'd smashed that bastard to the ground at least once while they were on the field together. Irritatingly, though, Notre Dame had won the game.

The governor repeated his earlier request. "Please sit," he said in a tone that made it sound more like a command.

Tom had not gotten where he was today by obeying commands. He continued to stand. "I still can't believe you shut us down. No warning. No work. No paychecks." Tom's Local 1953 ran the union for SpaceR's headquarters in Hawthorne. He leaned across the governor's desk. "Get your goons off the premises. Now." He spoke even more softly than the governor had, but he sounded even more like he was giving commands.

The Attorney General, seated a little out of the way, complained, "Tom, no need to get your nose out of joint. Everything's under control."

The governor chimed in, "You'll get your back pay, never fear. It's part of the deal we're demanding from that Toscano bastard."

Tom kept his eyes fixed on the governor as if the Attorney General did not exist. "We want our pay now."

The Attorney General, who did not like being disregarded, got out of his chair and came up beside the desk as well. "The governor said to stay cool. Your next payday is when…ten days from now?"

Tom nodded.

The Attorney General just smiled. "Relax, then. This will all be water under the bridge by that time. Toscano can't afford to keep you sidelined for that long. He'll pony up the cash, and you'll be back on the job. The only effect on your union members is, they'll have gotten a few days at the beach on SpaceR's dime."

Tom turned his glare slowly to the Attorney General. "So far none of your plans have worked out the way you expected. Why should this plan work any better than the last one?"

The governor answered, "Look, OK, you're right—we overplayed our hand when we tried to take their whole nest egg, so they built a new launch pad outside our jurisdiction." He paused.

Tom jumped in. "In ten days! They built a whole new pad in ten days! From scratch! In the middle of the goddam ocean!" Tom might have been famous for his collected calm, but sometimes events got the better of him anyway. He banged his fist against the desk. "What if he starts building the rockets out there too? Have you thought about that?"

The Attorney General scoffed. "Stop trying to make out the BrainTrust as a bunch of evil super-magicians. Sure, they managed to build a launch pad. But you tell me...how much more complicated is it to build a rocket?"

Tom looked mollified. A little bit. "Almost nothing made by humans is as complicated as a rocket." He thought about it some more. "Even if they had the tools, which they don't, where would they get the people with the experience needed to build them?"

Once in San Diego, Matt had also hopped a plane to LAX, then took a scruffy rideshare driver down to the Pizza

Show in Hawthorne. He walked in, slouched over as if he were a criminal trying to avoid being noticed for fear of capture. Which was, he thought, not all that far from the truth.

The aromas of the Pizza Show were warm and soothing. The place, so they claimed, had not changed since the days when the Beach Boys came in for pizza when they were still in high school.

Gary Schott sat in one of the red leather booths.

Gary was a senior worker on the rocket assembly line. He'd grown up building washing machines on a similar line back in Ohio, where he'd started his career jamming the hose onto the output port of the pump once every fourteen and a half seconds.

Since coming to SpaceR, he'd become one of the top utility infielders for rocket manufacturing. He'd learned just about every job, and if something went wrong or someone didn't show up, he was the one who filled in, fixed it up, and made it happen.

Gary was supremely competent, highly conscientious, and—the characteristic that best distinguished him in this situation—had considerable disdain for the union to which he belonged. He never got into physical or verbal battles with the diehard union members with whom he worked. When California had instituted the "card check" law for which the unions had lobbied so hard, which made every vote cast for/against unionization public, Gary had wisely voted for the union (unlike some of his more determinedly independent friends, whose accident rates on the job had mysteriously gone up after voting against the union). But Gary had been known, after a few beers, to observe among close friends that he would live better if he could disregard the union rules, focus on getting the job done, and keep his union dues in his retirement account, thank you very much.

Gary's chin was covered with salt-and-pepper stubble. He hadn't shaved since the governor had put the whole factory on an enforced vacation. He looked somber, though a twinkle lurked in his eyes. He raised an eyebrow at Matt as he sat down. "Slumming, Mr. Toscano?"

Matt shrugged. "I'm just Matt, Gary. I still remember you teaching me how the friction stir welding system works."

Gary nodded acknowledgment. "Good stuff. Good times."

"But every good technology gets replaced with something better, eventually. The next generation of Kestrel rockets is not going to need any welding."

Gary sat back against the plush booth back. "Really?"

Matt nodded. "Would you like to learn some new skills, or are you too old to learn any new tricks?"

Gary smiled broadly. "I think I still have a few new tricks left in me."

"Good. Oh, there is another problem. Would you be OK with making more money?"

For a moment Gary just stared at him. Then he flagged down a waitress. "Sounds like I should be celebrating. Can I buy you a beer?"

Matt chuckled. "You buy the beer, I'll buy the pizza." The waitress arrived, and Matt asked, "Does the special pizza still have meatballs?"

The waitress drawled, "Sure does, honey. Along with

pepperoni, mushrooms, bell peppers, olives, and Italian sausage."

Matt looked at Gary. "Will a large pizza be enough for the two of us?"

Gary nodded and ordered a pitcher, and the waitress left. Gary looked at Matt. "What's the catch?"

Matt winced. "You'll have to move to the new factory. Housing space is a little cramped at the moment. At first, you'll be sharing a room with three other workers. Even after we get everything shipshape, you won't be living in the suburbs anymore. Your next residence should be thought of as a really tiny condo three minutes' walk from the beach. And closer to the cafeteria, which has great seafood."

Gary pondered that. "Joyce would probably like that, since both kids are in college. The kids won't like losing the old home, but they'll live with it." He sighed. "So you're moving the whole thing to the BrainTrust? I can't say I'm surprised. The odds in the union betting pool are forty to sixty that you'd move the factory out there." He smiled. "Looks like I'm on the winning end."

Dash walked into Chance's office with puzzlement. "So what do you need that is urgent yet so secret you will not tell me what it is until I see you in person?" Dash was so focused on Chance that she did not see anything else in the office until she heard a chair scraping. She turned to see who it was and frowned. Dmitri.

Dmitri looked at her apologetically. "It's my fault. I

thought it best if we could arrange our meetings so that as few people as possible know that you're trying to help me with my upcoming assassination. I haven't even told my bodyguards." He paused. "It would be ironic and terrible if the Premier decided to use something other than polonium to kill me because he learned that you're working on a cure."

Dash raised an eyebrow. "Yes, I can see why extreme secrecy makes sense, and yet you seem to have taken Chance into your confidence." She looked at her intern. "Which is just as well, because I would very much like her help with the idea I have. I was going to ask you if I could bring her in on our project anyway."

Chance smiled an acknowledgment. "Thank you for trusting me, and believing in me." Her smile took on a mischievous gleam. "But there's another reason I wanted to see you, in addition to Dmitri's imminent death." She swiped a finger across the screen of her tablet. "I want to give you money."

Dash stared at her.

Dmitri chuckled. Chance joined him, then continued, "Well, Dmitri and I both want to give you money. And it's really Dmitri's money, when you get right down to it."

Dash's tablet beeped at her as the document Chance had flicked popped up. She studied it for a moment. "Custom Med Bays by Dash," she muttered. "I am afraid to ask what this is." She looked lower on the screen. "But whatever it is, you seem eager to give me a lot of money for it."

Dmitri roared with laughter. "The med bay you forced me to put on the *Buccaneer* is magnificent. Not only is it wonderful, but it was wondrously expensive. I've been telling my other friends with mega-yachts about it, and they all want one. Except, of course, they want one that's even better than mine."

Chance picked up the story. "So Dmitri came to me with a business proposition. He figured it would be hard to get you to sign up. And you have too much other work to do, anyway, not the least of which is a saving Dmitri's life. So I agreed to do the bulk of the design of the new med bays for these mega yachts."

Dmitri seemed eager to clarify. "You would get final sign-off authority, of course." He winced. "But what we really need is your name as part of the company title."

Chance nodded vigorously. "You're a brand now. The mega-yacht owners don't just want a wonderful suite of medical gear, they want a suite of medical gear designed specifically by you."

Dmitri looked at her anxiously. "So, will you do it?"

Dash rolled her eyes. "Do we not have more important things to worry about?" Both of the business partners looked at her anxiously, yet hopefully. She rolled her eyes again. "All right. Let me examine the terms of the agreement, but I expect I'll agree."

Dash put her tablet in her pocket and looked meaningfully at Dmitri. "Meanwhile, as I explained in my message to you, I have the first part of the plan for dealing with polonium poisoning in place." She reached into her other pocket and pulled out a bottle that rattled. It clearly contained pills. From the same pocket, she also pulled an electronic device. She held both out to Dmitri. "I was about to go looking for you, so I happen to have these with me."

She pulled up a chair and explained, "These pills contain a chelating agent, which is to say, a chemical that captures metal ions. I think I mentioned them before."

Dmitri grasped the bottle tightly like it was his last hope for life, and nodded. "So if I take these regularly, when the polonium is injected, this will capture all those atoms so they can't do any damage?"

Dash winced. "Not quite. As I also mentioned earlier, this is quite toxic. If the Premier waits long enough to attempt to kill you, these pills will kill you for him."

Chance raised an eyebrow. "So I guess it's extra-important for the Premier not to find out about this, lest he let you kill yourself on his behalf."

Dash frowned. "Just so. Unfortunately, there is more bad news."

Dmitri groaned. "It doesn't stop, does it?"

Dash plowed forward. "These pills, toxic as they are, will not save you. We can't put enough of the chelating agent in your blood on a continuous basis to capture all the polonium. The goal, rather, is to capture enough of the polonium and excrete it in your urine so that we can reliably detect the radiation with that detector." She pointed at the handheld she had given Dmitri along with the pills. "Then, within hours of when it's been administered, we can rush you in for treatment." She looked mournfully into Dmitri's eyes. "A treatment I am still working on. I know what must be done, and I am happy to have Chance working with me to build the machine we need."

Dmitri looked back and forth between the two of them. "So you're going to build a new machine just for me?"

Dash nodded. "Oh, yes." Her eyes brightened. "It will be

quite expensive. I am so happy you are willing to pay for it."

Dmitri blinked. "Ah. Of course. How good of me."

Chance put her hands on his shoulders and squeezed. "Given what a rocky start we had, we all have such a wonderful relationship now, don't you think?"

Dennis was listening to *Born to be Wild* as he relaxed in the driver's seat and watched his truck drive itself down I-40 across Arizona. He had a load of CPU chips straight from the Intel factory in Phoenix.

Dennis was a very happy owner-operator. Less than a year before he'd plunked down just about everything he had to buy his own truck. The rise of the California minimum wage to thirty dollars an hour had opened up great opportunities for the small entrepreneur. Trucks driven by employees of large trucking companies in the Red states were seized upon entering California for the crime of not paying minimum wage.

So virtually all goods were now shipped into California by independent truckers like himself. Since he was a business owner, not an employee, he was allowed to make less than minimum wage. The Teamsters Union in California had been lobbying to outlaw independent truckers ever since, claiming these small businesses were just regulatory evasions. However, the legislature, looking at the projections for the increased costs to the state's budget, had not yet relented.

The road from Kingman to the California border was a

seamless straight line across the desert, dotted with gnarly cholla cactus that looked, out of the corner of the eye, like skeletons on the parched earth.

Dennis was pretty sure that twenty years earlier the sparse vegetation was a little thicker and a little more green. The scientists in the Blue states said it had changed because of global warming. The President for Life's science advisor, speaking with the irrefutable scientific authority of a lawyer from the University of Tulsa College of Law, said that was ridiculous.

Dennis didn't know about that. He just knew that all things changed. Like the checkpoint on I-40 at the California border. When he'd first started making the trip, long before he'd bought his own truck, they had asked where he was coming from, just in case he was bringing oranges from Florida that might contain insects or diseases that might attack California's orchards. It had taken about eight seconds to roll through if you were coming from Phoenix.

That was something that had really changed. Now every truck's shipping manifest was scrutinized in minute detail. You were lucky to get through in an hour.

Of course, it was worse coming the other way, entering Arizona from California. The Arizona border patrol didn't care what you were shipping as long as you didn't have any illegal immigrants mixed in with the cargo. But they were fanatic about checking every nook, even if the nook were so small that only an illegal chihuahua would fit in the space.

They were all nuts.

Finally, the line of trucks trickled away until Dennis

was next. Dennis rolled down the window. "Howdy, officer," he offered as he handed over the manifest.

The cop took the manifest without a word, his lips pressed in a thin line. Dennis wondered who'd poked a stick up this guy's rear. That was another thing that had changed; long ago the cops had been friendly. Now more and more of them acted like this puckered jackass.

As the cop studied the manifest, his lips got even thinner. "You're carrying computer chips?"

Dennis nodded. "From Phoenix." In the old days, coming from Phoenix was the ticket to getting back on the road. Not today.

"And you're taking the chips to..."

Why was the guy asking questions that were answered by the paperwork? "San Francisco harbor. I guess they're loading the container directly on a ship."

The cop plucked his phone off his belt and started describing Dennis's cargo to someone he respectfully called, "Sir." Dennis started to sweat.

The cop waved a couple more cops over. "Please step out of the vehicle."

Dennis's heart jumped in his throat. As he opened the door, he asked, "What's wrong?"

The cop didn't respond until he was out of his truck and the door was closed. Dennis looked forlornly at his semi. At last, the cop explained, "Your cargo is heading to the BrainTrust for SpaceR. As you may have heard, the State of California is seizing all SpaceR assets. Your cargo is ours."

Dennis twisted his head so he could look at the paperwork. "But...the manifest says it's going to Goldman Sachs, not SpaceR." He thought desperately. "Don't the Goldman Sachs guys have a whole ship full of compute servers out there? Looks like these chips are going to them."

The cop loomed over Dennis, clearly uninterested in his opinion. "The bosses say the chips are going to SpaceR. Don't ask me how they know. I don't know. But I know these chips are ours now."

Dennis licked his lips. "OK. Can I drop the container off someplace for you?"

The cop shook his head. "Your vehicle is carrying forbidden goods. It belongs to us too. Civil forfeiture. We'll have someone come and take the truck in a few minutes."

Dennis couldn't breathe. "But...it's my truck. You can't take my truck. It's all I have, goddammit!" Dennis made the mistake of stepping closer to the cop with his fists closed. He was clubbed in the kidneys from behind. "You bastards!" he shrieked as he fell. So they clubbed him again.

He spent the night in jail in Needles. In the morning they gave him a breakfast of reconstituted eggs and cold oatmeal. With no truck, no savings, no job, and unable to apply for welfare benefits since he was not a resident of the state, the jail breakfast was the best thing he would eat for several weeks.

While Dennis ate his breakfast in jail, Matt sat down to a sumptuous repast at the cafeteria on board the *Haven*. Though calling the *Haven* dining area a cafeteria was a little like calling a diamond a chunk of coal. Plush carpets, suede booth benches, and sound absorbing walls and ceilings made it quiet even when crowded. He'd chosen eggs benedict and started eating with a healthy appetite.

Then he got a text message about Dennis's truck. He enjoyed his breakfast little more than Dennis.

Gina watched his expression change as he stopped eating and kept staring at the screen. "Trouble?" she asked. A tiny movement in his shoulders told her the rest. "Governor."

"CPU chips," Matt growled softly.

Gina shrugged. "Dash."

He dialed the phone. "Hey, Dash, you're not going to believe the problem we have now."

Dash offered Matt a chair in her office. "Sorry I could not come to *Argus*. I have a lot going on here on *Chiron*. Medical research, you know. Saving lives." She continued with a sob, "Or not saving them. Yesterday I had a candidate for rejuvenation that I had to reject because it would probably kill him. He died anyway this morning."

Matt's shoulders drooped. "I'm so sorry. I'd come back later, but…"

"But you have an emergency. Of course. I must say, SpaceR has brought a level of constant urgency to the BrainTrust that is perhaps healthy, however irritating it may be." She gestured for him to begin.

"Computer chips. You know modern rocketry is very dependent on real-time computer control of just about every aspect of the engines and flight geometry."

Dash nodded.

"The Great State of California has just snatched all the controller chips for the next gen Kestrels."

"I see." Dash paused, thinking. "As you may know, the BrainTrust does indeed manufacture chips under license from Intel, but they are always a couple of generations behind the newest and best. Our chips are used primarily by people and organizations that are worried about being hacked. We strip out the circuits for the government's backdoor."

Matt shook his head. "I'm not worried. Crazy as the California government is, even if the Reds in Washington were to give them access, I don't think they'd sabotage our rockets just to get back at us. Even *they* would view that as uncivilized." He thought about it. "Probably."

Dash responded, "You are probably right, although I suspect the risk is greater than you might guess. Regardless, the problem is that our chips supply fewer teraflops on a per-kilo basis than the newest chips. That could be a problem for you." She sighed, pulled out her tablet, and started doing some calculations. "Fortunately, our new titanium boosters are a little bit lighter than the old aluminum ones. I had thought that would be a pleasant surprise for you at the end, but I guess we could use the surplus weight budget for more chips to achieve the needed compute power."

Matt groaned. "So I'll need more chips. Let me guess—it's going to cost me more."

Dash laughed. "In fact, our chips, being of older designs, are easier to produce and cost less. You will be able to save some money on this." She paused then qualified her statement. "A little bit, anyway."

Matt whooped. "At last. It probably won't happen again, but it's a nice feeling while it lasts."

Gary listened as his friends checked in.

"No guards on the east fence."

"No guards on the north fence."

"Two guards on the main gate."

Everything looked to be about as Gary had expected. The governor may have locked the factory up, but his forces were hardly ready to stand up against any serious assault. Or any serious skullduggery, for that matter.

No guards could see what was about to happen. Gary spoke to the driver of the lead truck. "Bring up the lights." As Gary covered his eyes against the glare of the lead truck's headlights as he waved them forward. "Brandi, make a hole."

A woman in coveralls that hid her curves jumped to the chain link fence and started cutting. Two additional partners in crime went to help. Very quickly indeed they made a hole. The trucks, short-range haulers with electric motors, silently rolled over the metal plates they'd dropped on the gully-ridden dirt and into the east parking lot. As Brandi and the others set to work putting the fence back together, the trucks rolled up to a loading dock while another participant with the keys opened the adjacent door, entered, and started rolling the loading dock door up into the ceiling.

Word came from over the phone. "Stop a minute. The guards can hear you."

They stopped, and moments later the voice announced, "Ok, keep going. But *quietly*."

Brandi and her companions rejoined the main force. "Ok, everyone, you're all assigned specific pieces of equipment. Let's do this." The factory workers, now in the legally ambiguous state of burglars stealing their own equipment for the company that owned the gear, sped through the building to reach their specified targets. Equipment started to flow back to the dock and into the trucks.

Brandi snapped her chewing gum. "You know, boss, there's a really important piece of equipment we didn't put on the list."

Gary looked at her in puzzlement. She waved for him to follow her, across the factory floor, into the offices, out to the reception area. She pointed at the piece of critical gear.

Gary inhaled sharply. "Oh, yes. We *must* take this, even if we have to leave something else behind."

They brought back some of the crew who'd finished early and moved the gear ever so carefully out to the trucks. Everyone complimented Brandi on remembering the most important item in the factory.

They finished loading the trucks. Brandi stuck her gum to the dock, then stripped off her coveralls to reveal a black pantsuit with an ivory blouse and a blue scarf. As they rolled up to the guards, she swung down from the passenger side of the first truck's cab. "Gentlemen," she called out, "Let us through."

One guard strolled over, peering at her suspiciously.

"What the hell are you doing here? Nobody in, nobody out, by order of the governor."

Brandi, using the expression she usually used to fend off jerks with crude pickup lines, quite similar to the expression she'd used when giving commands as an Air Force lieutenant, waved her hands around at the trucks and the gate. "Yet, as you can see, we already came in. I'm just following orders, just like you. It took us longer to load this stuff than expected." She shrugged. "Sorry."

The second guard came over. "What's going on?"

Brandi jumped in before the first guard could answer. "Moving some key items to more secure storage. Trust me when I tell you the boss wants this stuff as secure as possible. Relax, boys, it's not like we could pack the whole factory into two trucks." She pulled out some paperwork. "Look, I've got a shipping manifest here; the stuff we're taking. I'll sign it and give it to you as a receipt." She wrote her name on the top sheet with a flourish and handed it to them. "Now, can we go? We've got a long night ahead of us."

The guards looked at each other skeptically, and Brandi blew out a breath in exasperation. "Let me show you what we've got." She led them to the back of the truck, opened the door, and let them see the most important prize of the journey. Her voice took on a honey-coated drawl. "Does this look like it's gonna help that SpaceR creep build more rockets? Nobody's said so, but I presume the big boss will want to put this in his reception area. Sort of a way of giving the other guy the finger."

Finally, one guard muttered to the other, "She's right, this ain't gonna help nobody build no rocket ships."

The other guard shook his head. "This is the strangest assignment I've ever had." He looked at the receipt Brandi had given him and waved the other man into the gatehouse. "Open it." He turned and tipped his cap to Brandi. "You have a nice night, ma'am."

Brandi smiled. "You too."

She hopped back in the truck.

Gary took off. He raised an eyebrow. "What was that again? 'That creep at SpaceR?'"

Brandi switched off the honey-coated drawl; she was once again all Air Force officer. "Can it, airman."

Gary sat up straighter. "Yes, ma'am!" He slumped back down. "Or should that be, 'Aye, aye, ma'am'? We're living on a ship, after all."

After spending the night driving, the day on the ferry, and another night hauling the equipment into place in the *Argus*, Gary and Brandi stood with their crew on the promenade of the manufacturing ship. As Matt approached they all beamed at him, blocking his way.

Matt looked around at all the shining faces. "What's up?"

Gary answered, "Special equipment arrival, Mister CEO. Let me show you what we've got." He handed Matt the manifest.

Matt scanned through the pages at high speed, muttering an occasional, "great," or "thank God!" He looked up in astonishment. "These are all the most critical items we couldn't replicate here. Where'd you get all this stuff?"

Gary looked at the ground for a moment. "We, ah, made an informal arrangement to move them from Hawthorne to more secure storage."

Brandi snickered. "Very informal."

Matt was clearly having trouble deciding whether to frown about the theft, laugh about the escapade, or commend them on their initiative.

Brandi interrupted his musings. "The most important item isn't on the list."

A mutter of agreement arose throughout the small crowd of desperadoes. Mystified, Matt followed as Brandi led them into the new reception area by the executive offices. She raised her hand. "Ta-da!"

Matt looked up. A life-size suit of armor stood before him, slightly larger than a man. It was dark cherry red and SkyBlast yellow, with Black Widow's autograph over the heart.

Matt's eyes misted over and he looked at his henchmen with unblinking respect. "By far the most important piece of equipment from the old factory," he whispered. "Consider yourselves all put in for bonuses." His expression turned wry. "Assuming we still have a company in four months—let's be clear."

9

FUXING RISING

Devise and run a Nigerian Hoax, as described in the preceding module, against your teammates and teachers. Extra merit tokens awarded for a successful hoax. Merit rewards deducted for running the hoax against your parents or others.

—Accel, Topic: Mental Manipulation. Module: Nigerian Hoax Wrap-up

The combined fleets of the Fuxing and Prometheus archipelagos came upon their destination—an empty point in the ocean equidistant from China, Taiwan, and the Philippines—as the sun peeked over the horizon. The immense bulks of the isle ships cast shadows stretching to the horizon. Caught in those shadows, a peculiar cluster of disparate boats awaited them.

Ping stood with the other project leaders on the *Taixue* near the forward gangway of the promenade deck. She shook her head as she looked down at the vessels. "Sampans! Riverboats. What kind of an idiot would bring a sampan out here? It's a miracle they made it."

Jam pointed out the obvious. "I'd guess about half of them *didn't* make it. See how many people are crammed on board? They must've rescued the people from the boats that sank." She continued with admiration in her voice, "My kind of people."

Lenora tapped on her phone. "Captain Ainsworth? Are you planning to dock the sampans first? If you don't, they'll founder. It'd be a shame if they all drowned so close to their destination." She hung up. "I'd hoped for a turnout like this from the desperately poor who passed the Accel assessment intro, braving all obstacles to reach us." She bit her lip. "But it was probably a mistake sending out the app before we got here. Hope we didn't lose anyone."

Ciara pointed to starboard at a mega-yacht that seemed intent on picking off as many of the sampans as it could as it hurried to dock. "Not *everyone* had to suffer to get here, it looks like," she observed dryly.

Lenora smiled. "Ah, yes. That would be the princelings. Hopefully our first paying students."

Ping stared at Lenora. "You were expecting them?"

Lenora nodded. "A college student named Liu Fan Hui sent a message alerting me they'd be meeting us." Lenora waved to the mega-yacht, where two young men and one young woman stood on the top deck peering through the shadows at them. The female saw her and waved back.

Ping half-jumped. "Liu Fan Hui? Are you sure?"

Lenora looked at her, puzzled. "Quite sure. Know her?"

Ping seemed to need a moment to regain her composure. Finally, she growled, "I don't have to know her. Princelings. Trouble."

Ciara explained for her mother, "Money. Revenue."

Jam thought a distraction might be in order. "What about the other ship? The one with the advertisement on the side."

Lenora offered a guess. "Probably a charter. Someone with money."

Ping added, "But someone without a daddy in the Politburo. Someone without connections. No mega-yacht for him."

Lenora looked at her shrewdly. "A self-made man. Excellent."

Adam no longer remembered his real name. He'd had so many names and identities that the original had been lost to history. For now he was Adam, because his passport said so.

Of course, here on the BrainTrust he had to remember his current name without recourse to a passport, because you didn't need a passport. Or a driver's license. Or a birth certificate. The closest thing most people had to an ID was their company key badge, used for getting into the locked office if you felt inspired to get some work done at midnight when no one was around. Or, in the startups where everyone was working at midnight, for getting in at noon when no one was around.

Adam fingered his SpaceR key badge as he opened the door into the double-decker 3D printing hall. A half-complete rocket booster for the new Kestrel Titan gleamed dully at him. He'd heard rumors they were going to soup up the outer surface, make it pretty, but today it still looked like silver-grey titanium.

He pulled out his tricorder—really a Bluetooth hacking remote, but it looked like a tricorder—and walked slowly around the rocket, detecting and infiltrating the controller chips one by one. In a few minutes, he was done. All the controller chips had been patched with whatever code his boss had chosen to upload. Unbelievably easy.

Since hooking up with his new boss, all his jobs had been unbelievably easy. The tricorder hacked through everything like a ninja zooming through an open window. It was as if the tricorder had the American government's master keys to the backdoors in all the chips. After the first half dozen jobs, he'd concluded the tricorder did, in fact, have those master keys.

Realizing he wielded the ultimate weapon for world domination, Adam had of course tried to use the tricorder and its magic to pull off several jobs of his own, but the box refused to yield its secrets or use them for any purpose other than the jobs downloaded from his boss's web site. X-ray analysis showed the tricorder more than ready to destroy its most sensitive components if Adam attempted a physical breach. Disappointing, but thrilling in its own way. Either his boss, whoever he was, had stolen the famous seven-key code from the US government, or Adam was working more or less directly for the Chief Advisor, or even the President for Life. If so, he was a patriot even if he were also a saboteur.

Adam verified that his device had recorded verifications on all the hacks on all the chips before departing. When he uploaded those verifications for the boss, payment would appear as if by magic in his account. He loved being a patriot, particularly when it was so profitable.

Lenora briefly surveyed her domain, namely, her classroom. At the head of the room, a small circle of chairs sat on a plush carpet that covered most of the floor. Four teamwork areas occupied the rest of the room. Three of the areas held collections of apparatus like you would expect to find in a lab. One area surrounded a table with a collection of boxes of the shape and style that one might expect to hold board games. The lighting came soft and subdued from the entire ceiling. Acoustic tiles covered those sections of the walls not covered in display screens. The tiles and the carpet subdued the sound so successfully that the four teamwork areas and the circle of chairs could all be alive with people without the noise from one group disturbing other teams. In a ship that would someday soon teem with families and every square foot of floor space was precious, the room's spaciousness seemed extravagant.

She sat down at the head of the circle of chairs and hunched over her tablet, and soon a bot escorted the three princelings from the mega-yacht to her. Lenora rose to greet them. The woman who led the princelings was taller in person than she had seemed when viewed across the ocean. And she wore calm confidence like armor. Lenora knew by looking at her that if she cried, which she would not, her makeup would not run...if she wore makeup, which she did not.

Liu Fan Hui smiled as she stepped forward, though the smile did not reach her eyes. "I am Liu Fan Hui," she said as she extended her hand in greeting.

Lenora nodded. "Yes, the daughter of a Politburo member."

"Just so." Fan Hui pointed to the tall young man who was at that moment carefully studying his perfectly manicured fingernails. "This is Guang Jian, son of the third member of the Standing Committee." Guang Jian shifted his head slightly in what might have been an acknowledgment. Fan Hui pointed to the other male member of the group, a short fellow with pimply skin whose hair stuck out in ragged, unkempt patches despite obvious attempts to rein it in. "Chen Ying, another son of the Politburo."

Lenora nodded. "Your message reached me that you were on your way. Welcome to the BrainTrust."

Guang raised an eyebrow. "This is not really the Brain-Trust. This is the Fuxing, correct?"

Lenora tilted her head side to side. "Both, really. I suppose a detailed characterization would be, we are standing in the isle ship *Taixue*, one of two ships currently of the Fuxing archipelago, a wholly owned subsidiary of the BrainTrust Consortium. The Fuxing may be either an archipelago or a fleet, depending on whether we're at anchor or moving."

Fan Hui looked puzzled. "Only two ships? I saw several more than that. What are the others?"

Lenora answered, "The other three ships belong to the Prometheus archipelago, though they'll be staying here for a while we all help build a third Fuxing ship. We originally had another ship, but our third ship got hijacked." At the surprised expressions on the three students, she clarified, "No, not by pirates. By the Consortium, as the launch pad for SpaceR."

Chen's eyes widened. "Cool. I watched the first launch. Will we get the chance to work with SpaceR?" Seeing impatience in the expressions of both Fan and Guang, Chen waved it away. "Whatever. We'd like to be the first students in your university."

Lenora brought her hands together, not quite clapping. "Excellent. We do of course have some tests you'll need to pass. I presume you can all afford the tuition, room, and board."

Guang drew himself up to his full height. "We have to pass a test? Are you kidding? You have an empty ship with no students. You need us more than we need you."

Fan stroked Guang's arm soothingly as she spoke to Lenora. "Of course, Ms. Thornhill. We'll be happy to take your tests." She glared at her boyfriend. "It won't be a problem. When do we begin?"

Lenora pondered for a moment. "Give me an hour to get set up. In the meantime, let's assume you'll pass." *As you already take for granted*, she thought with amusement. Her thoughts turned sour. They would in fact almost certainly pass, and she *did* need them as much or more than they needed her. Guang had an irritatingly sharp mind, even if, as she suspected, he were lazy, cynical, self-centered, and completely amoral.

Hopefully, they needed her as much as she needed them. For them to have come here, they must have had few options. Princelings would not go to a university that was not already prestigious unless serious problems lurked in their histories. "I'll have a bot show you to your cabins, and have your belongings delivered there."

The soft sound of an orchestral symphony came from the Chief Advisor's tablet, telling him he had good news. A quick glance told him the story. His viruses had been uploaded to all the controller chips in the Kestrel Titan booster. When launched, the booster would dance to his tune.

His tune was simpler than the launch plan intended by SpaceR. Under the Advisor's control, the rocket would lift off, tilt quickly to its side, roar over the BrainTrust archipelago, and transform into a fireball.

As the devastation swept over the BrainTrust, the Advisor's Navy ships, humbly standing by just outside the archipelago's reef in case of emergency, would move in to render aid. One team would have special instructions—to render aid to the isle ship *Chiron*, regardless of how much or how little damage she'd taken. They would sweep through the vessel to seek out and render aid specifically to Dr. Dash. In an emergency like this, Dash would surely be in the hospital emergency trauma area helping victims. The Advisor's team would scoop her up and, amidst the confusion, transport her with all due haste to America.

The Advisor was only slightly concerned that Dash would be killed in the rocket blast. Some of the newer isle ships, he'd heard, were built primarily with magnesium, and could easily wind up turning into fiery immolations of their own. But the *Chiron* was an older ship made with tough, reliable steel. She'd survive, and he would have her.

He savored the moment, contemplating idly which ships he'd send for the event. The cruiser *Vella Gulf* was already tasked with shadowing the BrainTrust ships. He'd send the *Harper's Ferry*, which was designed for docking, relief, and rescue operations. Everyone would be surprised if he didn't send an actual support vessel, and they might suspect that his motives were not honorable.

And he'd send the *Zumwalt*. The *Zumwalt* had been intended to be the first of thirty-two ships of a new, advanced class of guided missile destroyer. Fabulous cost overruns had reduced the scope of development to just three ships. Since the *Zumwalt's* guns had been designed to fire a very advanced artillery shell, which had also had to be canceled because of its own cost overruns, the Navy was constantly seeking missions for the ship to prove it had not been a waste of money.

Designed to support shore and landing operations in addition to deep-water combat, the *Zumwalt* could actually perform well in the Advisor's new mission…as long as they didn't wind up in a firefight with the Russian or Chinese ships annoyingly hanging around in the area.

Yes, the *Zumwalt*, the *Harper's Ferry*, and the *Vella Gulf* would do nicely.

It was good to have a simple, reliable plan in place at last.

Fleet Captain Jack Ainsworth stood on the bridge listening to Lenora Thornhill and looking out the window at the yacht cradled against the side of their isle ship. He was not impressed by her words. "You want me to do what?"

Lenora repeated herself. "I want you to be the scientist in the first test we put these princelings through." She touched him on the shoulder. "It won't be very hard. I'll feed you your lines through an earbud. Just simple things like 'turn the voltage up to fifty,' and 'you must do this for me and for science.' Oh, and you have to act very authoritatively. Which is to say, you just have to act like yourself. You *are* the captain, after all. And you are very good at looking very authoritative." She smirked at his look of frustration. "But you'll have to put on that posh upper-class accent of yours. Fan and Guang were at Cambridge. To sound authoritative to them, best if you sound authoritatively British."

Jack's eyes glowed with mischief. He started to speak, but Lenora knew what was coming.

She waved an accusatory finger at him. "And don't try laying it on thick, Mister Fleet Captain. You were born in Durham, not a brewery. The same place Tony Blair grew up, for heaven's sake." She shook her head. "Honestly, I don't understand why we ever let men run anything. *Children.*"

Her glare turned into a smirk. "And you'll also have to look very grave, ever so scholarly, and deeply analytical. Those might challenge you a bit more."

Jam interceded when the captain looked like smoke might come from his ears. "I'm quite sure the captain can pull it off. He did an excellent job of looking very cold and analytical the first time I met him." Jam had wondered why Lenora wanted her to come along for this conversation, and now she understood. Lenora obviously knew she had history with the captain. Jack had first met her after his bosun had found her hiding as a stowaway on his ferry.

Foolishly, Jack refused to surrender to the two women without more fight. "I still don't see why you can't do this yourself. You have all the characteristics you just described, Lenora. And to top it off, you really *are* a scientist."

Lenora chuckled. "And for many of the student candidates, I *will* play that role. Although just to be clear, most scientists would be horrified to hear you accuse me of being one of them. I'm just a teacher, Jack." She paused. "But to answer your question, while I can probably do a perfectly adequate job of being stern, commanding, and scientific for the many students we hope to receive from rural communities, these are *princelings*. And even though a couple of members of the Politburo are women, China is still a patriarchal society. We'll have to use every trick in the book to persuade these tyrants in training that we have authority over them. And for the test, that is crucial. So you, my male friend, are up to bat."

Jack grunted. "So what do I have to do?"

"It would be best for you to learn by seeing how it's done. My daughter, as it happens, is about to run the test with our first candidate from the sampans."

Jack looked puzzled. "I thought anybody with the combination of foolishness, chutzpah, and insanity to make that horrific trip was assured a place on the ship. At least, that was the way it worked with the BrainTrust and the stowaways on my ferry." He smiled at Jam since the last stowaway he had dealt with was the Pakistani commando.

Jam smiled back, and a flash of warm kinship passed between them. She beckoned him. "I was helping Ciara set up earlier. Shall we go see how she does?"

Matt pulled the brim of his hat lower to protect his eyes from the sun. He stood outside Port Freeport, south of Houston, and watched with a complicated blend of satisfaction, irritation, and sorrow as his trucks rolled up to the docks.

He felt satisfied because he knew that the rockets and rocket parts he was shipping from SpaceR's facilities in Texas would not be intercepted by the Great State of California. He felt irritated because detouring around California (and California's best friend, Oregon) made his life both complicated and expensive. Simply going through Mexico or Canada would entail paying a thirty-five percent tariff, imposed by those nations on US exports when the USA had imposed such tariffs on them. Aargh.

If it were summer, he'd ship the equipment through the Northwest Passage, up and around Canada. Packed solid with thick ice for thousands of years, the passage had opened in the summer of 2013, and had opened every summer since then. Decades later it was open six months of the year. But today they were in the middle of the six months during which the Passage was closed.

So he'd settled on shipping through the Panama Canal.

They too had imposed a tariff on American goods, but not as big a tariff as Mexico's. Good enough.

Finally, Matt felt sorrow because of the endless weeds in the cracked and broken asphalt of the parking lots where long ago thousands of cars had waited to be loaded for export. He remembered coming here once as a child, seeing those lots jammed to the edges with Ford F-Series pickup trucks. In those days the Ford pickup was the largest-selling vehicle in the world. He remembered having a soft pain in his gut the first time he saw a Ford advertisement, instead of saying "Largest-selling vehicle in the world," instead announce proudly, "Largest-selling vehicle in America." He'd known in some visceral way that something wonderful had been lost that day.

Well, no matter. Things were looking up for Freeport. It seemed likely he'd be shipping gear back and forth with the BrainTrust through here for some time to come.

In fact, it took them a few minutes more than expected to get ready to test the first student, Jun Laquan. After a couple of minutes of conversation in the observation room, Ciara and Lenora agreed that Lenora would in fact be the scientist for this run while Ciara gave a running explanation of what was going on for the captain and Jam. Jam tried to excuse herself, but as dirtside expedition leader, Lenora explained, she would have to understand all this stuff even though she wouldn't be doing it. Lenora shrugged a lab coat on over her business suit and went to meet the parents and the boy who would be the true subject of the test.

Jun Laquan knew he had wide, bright eyes because his mother told him so all the time. He stood by her side while he clung to his father on the other. He trembled slightly, though he knew he should behave more in a more manly fashion, as befit a fourteen-year-old. He tried very hard to pay close attention to the woman wearing the white lab coat, although his fear made it hard for him to concentrate. The scientist was the cause of part of his fear. He had never seen anyone like her. She was Western, and very stern. Her name was Dr. Thornhill.

Dr. Thornhill explained that she was going to give him some tests in a little while, but first, she needed his help conducting an experiment for someone else. The experiment would have no impact on his acceptance on the *Taixue*, but she needed him to follow instructions. He nodded gravely, wondering why she needed his help. Unbidden, she explained the plan. In the experiment, they would use electricity to enhance learning. He should not worry, she reiterated. All he had to do was follow directions, and all would be well.

Sitting in the observation room with Jam and Ciara, watching Lenora and Jun on multiple vidcams, Jack shook his head and growled, "This is already a screwup. There is no way the boy will believe that his performance during this experiment will not impact his acceptance."

Ciara sighed. "How right you are," she said gloomily. "It's a serious problem, but we haven't figured out how to fix it. The good news is that the final outcome of this test is not the main measurement. In fact, it's the least of the indicators." She pointed at screens around their observation room. "We depend more upon these than the final conclusion of the experiment."

Jack only recognized a couple of the readouts. One looked to be a heartbeat that was racing. "It occurs to me that this room looks more like a surgeon's operating room than a simple observation station."

Ciara chirped, "More than you know. We have Jun Laquan hooked up on sensors so exotic you'd never find them in surgery. 3D EEG, micro-expressions, pupil dilations, toe twitches, and stomach contractions, as well as the usual blood pressure, heartbeat, and galvanic skin response. It all feeds into our evaluation process."

Back in the experimental room, Jun listened as the scientist explained more about his duties. Jun would sit at the control panel and ask the experimental subject a series of questions. The subject was a man in an adjacent room separated from the control room by a big glass window. When the subject gave the right answer, Jun would simply go on to the next question. If the subject got the answer wrong, Jun would raise the voltage using the dial on the panel, and press the button that would give the subject an electric shock. Again, the scientist explained, the boy had nothing to fear because she would be standing right there supervising at all times. This did nothing to calm Jun's fear.

As Jun sat down at the panel with the voltage dial and the stimulator button, he looked through the window at the subject, who sat in a chair with his back to Jun's window. Jun could see that the man's arms were strapped to the chair. Jun wondered briefly why he and the man were not allowed to see each other's faces, but the scientist seemed uninterested in answering questions, so Jun swallowed the desire to ask.

Jun also wondered why, at the halfway point, the dial face changed from white to red. He wanted to ask about that too, but he was pretty sure he knew the answer. These voltages were dangerous. They could not only hurt the man but probably kill him.

At first, everything went well. Jun would ask a question, and the subject would give him the right answer. But as time went on and the questions got harder, the man started making mistakes. Jun had to turn up the voltage again and again. Soon, the man started crying out in pain every time Jun touched him with electricity. Jun started trembling. He asked the scientist if she could get someone else to do this, but her voice, while still calm and gentle, remained stern and insistent.

Jun started to think that he should stop anyway. He remembered that the scientist had assured him that his performance helping her would not impact his admission. However, he had a terrible suspicion that if he stopped he would be rejected, and the long, terrible trip his parents had taken to bring him here, the trip that had cost them everything, would be wasted.

Ainsworth paced back and forth. "We have to put a stop to this."

Jam stood and peered at one of the displays. "What about the man being electrocuted? Someone really volunteered for that? Tell me what's really going on here, or I'm going to break him out now."

Ciara made a placating gesture. "No! There's no electricity involved. Jun's control panel is a dummy. The fellow in the electric chair is an actor. He's just following his script. He'll introduce himself to Jun when the test is over and show him no harm was done."

The captain stopped pacing. "Still, what it's doing to Jun..." He pointed a finger at Ciara. "And you go along with this? You're going to do this to children on your ships as well?"

Ciara slumped into a defensive position. "For what it's worth, there's an automatic shutoff for the test if the sensors indicate the subject may reach a state of severe overstress."

Ainsworth bellowed, "Then why isn't it shutting down?"

Ciara pondered the displays. Wonderingly, she answered, "Because Jun is demonstrating exceptional resilience. Really exceptional. I think he may... Well, we'll know soon."

She clasped her hands tightly together. "It's still terrible.

When Mom first explained what she wanted me to do, I told her absolutely not, no way, period end."

Jack waited for a moment for her to escape the deep funk she had fallen into and continue. When she did not, he prompted, "And?"

Ciara grinned ruefully. "And she clapped, and congratulated me on having passed the test." Her grin turned thoughtful, then irritated. "Then she explained to me in that calm determined way she has why I had to do it."

Ciara rose, held out her hands, wet her lips, and rendered a beautiful imitation of her mother's voice. "How much do you think this little expedition cost, Jack? The ships, the equipment, the immersive educations that will go on for years before they pay off. Unless our students are creative enough, determined enough, and honorable enough to build—not to steal, but to build—at least two multi-billion-dollar businesses, this archipelago will fail. But if we succeed, more archipelagos will follow, each one cheaper than the last as our tech advances. Each one able to take on more people even though they may be less exceptional, until, at last, all people can be welcomed."

Ciara wilted for a moment, exhausted by playing her mother. Then she straightened to assume the role once more. "If we succeed, thousands of isle ships will enable millions of people to escape the corrupt, vicious, and bigoted governments and cultures that now trap and oppress them. But if we fail, there will never be another archipelago like this. We *must* make sure that each and every last student has the characteristics and the tools necessary to make our mission here succeed."

The ghost of her mother left her. Exhausted but once again herself, Ciara frowned ruefully. "So here I am."

By the time Jun had turned up the electricity to the point where the dial moved into the red zone, the man was begging him to stop. And Jun knew several things. He knew his parents would be very disappointed if he were rejected from the Fuxing archipelago, and he also knew that his parents would be very upset and angry if he hurt this man. And he knew, because of what his parents had taught him, that to continue would be wrong.

He was not going to press the button again. He and his parents would be shipped away, and soon they would be standing on some dock in some port in China with no money and no place to go. He turned away from the dial and the button and wailed and cried uncontrollably. "I won't do it," he mumbled between sobs of despair.

A broad smile lit Lenora's face. "I never would have expected such bravery from our very first student." She knelt before him and put her arms around him. "Congratulations. You have passed the most difficult test. You and your parents are guaranteed a place here." She waved to the cameras. "Lead in the parents." As the door swung open she rose, still touching the boy on his shoulder, and spoke to the parents. "You have a marvelous son here. I expect to see him do great things with us."

The parents beamed, and the father spoke first. "I knew it. I knew he was supposed to be more than just a rural farmer." He stood somehow straighter. "My son will be a great man."

The mother, seeing the tears still streaming down Jun's face, helped him up and spoke with alarm. "Are you OK?" She turned to Lenora. "What did you do to him?"

Lenora took a deep breath. "I did not hurt him physically, but I put him under terrible mental stress. I'm very sorry. But it was necessary."

The captain bellowed, "Necessary? It was entirely *un*necessary!"

Ciara touched the skipper lightly on the arm. "Remember the big picture."

The captain glared down at her and started to speak, but then Lenora entered the room. She seemed to know what he would say just with a glance at his eyes, and she stepped on his words.

She moved into the captain's personal space and a fire rose in her eyes. "You can help me or not, but these tests will go forward. We will select the best and the brightest, and they will succeed, and this archipelago will crush the barriers to human progress and bring light and hope to every impoverished corner of this planet."

The captain glared back, but Ciara pulled on his sleeve. "Just go with the program, Captain Ainsworth. You already passed this test earlier."

He looked down at her, astonished. "When?"

Ciara threw up her hands. "Who knows? But you're the fleet captain, right? You think you could've become fleet captain without my mother's consent?"

The captain looked at her, disturbed, then looked back at Lenora. "What did you do to me?"

Lenora stepped back and gave him a smug smile. "What difference does it make? My daughter's right, you know. Just get with the program. It'll all be all right." Nodding goodbye to Jam, she wrapped her hands around one of his arms while her daughter wrapped her hands around the other. "I promise."

As Jack allowed the women to walk him to his doom, he wondered what test they had him in the middle of right now. Was he passing, or failing? His thoughts were not calmed by the realization that the answer was surely "both."

Jam sat in the observation room, shivering ever so slightly with unused adrenaline, watching Ciara and Lenora lead the captain away. "This is not acceptable," she muttered to herself. Her BFF's words rose unbidden to her lips. "It must be improved upon." Listening as this insistent thought echoed in her mind, she brightened. Of course. She pulled out her cell phone. "This *will* be improved upon."

RADIOACTIVE

The unavoidable price of reliability is simplicity.
—Tony Hoare

Dmitri could no longer decide which he hated more, going to the bathroom to pee or taking the tablets Dash demanded he ingest every four hours throughout the day. He supposed he hated going to the bathroom more, because his fingers trembled a bit as he took the urine sample to put it in the beta radiation detector. The trembling invariably caused him to make a mess of the process. Urine everywhere.

Moreover, the trembling was not caused by his fear of finding radiation. Rather, the trembling was caused by the pills. Intellectually, he understood that he should hate taking the pills because they were the cause of the trembling that caused the problem with the urine. His emotional reaction, however, led him to hate the moment when the consequences came into play. When he was in the bathroom. Turning philosophical for a moment, he realized that much of the troubled history of mankind was a consequence of similar emotional overrides of intellectual understanding.

Of course, the trembling fingers were not the only symptom of the chelating agents poisoning his bloodstream. He usually felt a strong desire to vomit about an hour after taking the pills. All in all, he just wished the Premier would hurry up and poison him and be done with it.

He finally got the urine-soaked pad into the device. It promptly set off a wailing alarm and started blinking a red light, fast and furious. At that moment, Dmitri realized he had been kidding himself. In reality, he would have much preferred for the Premier to take his time about killing him.

He lay in the bed hooked to dozens of sensors as activity swept around him. Dmitri asked the question of no one in particular, "So, do I have a chance?"

Both Chance and Dash paused in their frenetic dance with the machine that had just been wheeled into the room. It was not like any machine he'd ever seen before. He suspected this was the special machine for which he'd paid the development costs. Dash answered him first. "Of course you have a chance, Dmitri. I have not spent the past weeks poisoning you with chelating agents for the fun of it."

Chance interrupted, "Oh, Dash, be honest now. You've had some fun poisoning Dmitri, at least a little bit."

Dash pursed her lips. "Not very much."

Chance pulled a cluster of thin tubes from the new machine as Dash wheeled it into position beside him. Chance waved the tubes, each with a shiny long needle at the end, in front of him. "So we made this, the vampire filter, just for you. We're going to stick needles into each of your major arteries and flush your blood through the system as fast as we can, filtering out both the chelating agents and the polonium as fast as we can pump." She turned to her companion. "Dash, I'll let you give Dmitri the bad news."

Dash rolled her eyes. She placed a hand on Dmitri's shoulder. "I am very sorry. This is going to hurt a great deal."

Dmitri's eyes went wide. "Couldn't you—" he grunted as Chance slid the first needle home. "Couldn't you—" Dash slid in the next needle.

It took all his concentration not to jump as if zapped by electrodes as the women hooked him up to the vampire.

Dash spoke apologetically. "I would anesthetize you, but with the filter running at full speed, flushing your blood clean, it would be quite ineffective."

Chance chimed in, "And besides, she's enjoying this. At least a little bit." Dash glared at her.

The vampire went to work, and Dmitri watched his life's blood drain from every part of his body at the same time. He felt lightheaded.

Chance frowned. "Oh, that's not good."

Dash pursed her lips again. "I told you it needed more testing."

Chance looked at Dmitri and explained, "We don't seem to be able to pump the blood back into you as fast as we're pulling it out. It should be OK, though. If you pass out, there's no need for you to feel any anxiety."

Dash shook her head. A few moments later, she pressed the button, and the whir of the machine changed. "OK, we are done for the moment. You should be feeling better any time now."

Dmitri nodded. "I don't feel faint anymore. I guess I have most of my blood back again?"

Both women were watching the readouts on the vampire too closely to pay attention. Finally, the machine stopped making any noise at all. Chance spoke. "That's it."

Dmitri smiled. "That's it? We're done? Great!"

Dash shook her head. "I am afraid this is only the beginning."

For the first time, Chance also spoke with sorrow. "Dash is right. We won't really know we're done until we know we're done. We're breaking new ground here. You'll go down in the history books." She paused. "One way or the other."

Dmitri gave them a weak smile. "Could we at least take out those needles? Quickly, perhaps?"

Dash responded mournfully, "I am sorry. We will have to do this again in about half an hour, to see how much of the polonium we can get as it's excreted from the cells." She closed her eyes. "And then we'll see how much damage the polonium has done to you in the brief time it was in your system before we extracted it." She paused. "So we need to leave the needles in."

Dmitri responded with proper Russian philosophy. "Well, it's not as bad as simply dying. The pain reminds you that you're still alive."

———

Wolf brought Aar along with him to the gangway from the *Dreams Come True* to the *Haven*. He was looking for Dash, since the dispatcher had told him that she had requested him. Wolf was eager to see her again since they'd had so much fun together the first time, but the woman they found wearing the white lab coat was too tall to be Dash.

When they walked up to her, she turned to them and smiled. "Hi. I'm Chance. You must be Wolf and Aar. Dash told me how you'd helped her after she left us on Dmitri's yacht. She thought you could help me find the assassin who tried to murder our current patient."

Aar's eyes widened. "Is your patient all right?"

Chance waved a hand in a gesture of uncertainty. "Not clear yet. It's still a coin flip."

Wolf smacked his left fist into his right palm. "Dash is living up to her reputation of getting people into exciting situations. Do you know who the assassin is? Can we just take him, or do we have to figure out who he is first?"

Chance pulled an instrument from her pocket. "First we have to find him, but I expect that not to be a problem."

Chance led them through the *Haven* to Dmitri's suite with the confident stride of someone who knew where she was going and had been there many times before.

As they hustled, Aar commented with puzzlement, "Didn't this guy try to kidnap you and Dash? It *is* the same guy, right?"

Chance acknowledged this. "Yeah, but we worked it out. Now we're business partners."

Wolf chortled. "Only on the BrainTrust." More seriously, he continued, "So you said it wouldn't be a problem finding the perp. But you don't know who it is yet, which suggests you don't have any useful video of the attack. Do you have a trick up your sleeve, or are you simply a next-generation Sherlock Holmes?" He pointed at the slim little gadget in her hand. "Does it have to do with that?"

Chance nodded. "It certainly does." She tapped the device. "This is a very sensitive beta radiation detector. Dmitri was poisoned with polonium."

Wolf grunted. "So the Russian Union Premier is at it again."

"We presume so," Chance responded. "Anyway, properly contained polonium is virtually impossible to detect, but once you pull it out of the bottle to use it, you inevitably leak enough residue to create a radioactive trail."

They reached Mikhailov's dwelling. The door was locked but Chance swept through unhindered, causing Wolf to raise an eyebrow.

Yefim and Gleb were both in the entryway living room, pacing with anxiety. Gleb was the first to ask, "How is our boss? Will he be OK?"

Chance spoke cheerfully. "Oh, he's fine. You know, he asked Dash specifically if she could save him from polonium poisoning while we were in mediation."

Aar laughed out loud. "Cheeky bastard, asking his victim to save his life."

Wolf smiled broadly. "But of course she agreed."

Chance nodded. "Of course she did. He's recovering nicely."

Wolf watched the reactions of all the people in the room to this pronouncement. Aar looked puzzled since she'd given a considerably more negative assessment earlier. Yefim looked relieved. Gleb looked like he'd been struck by lightning. Wolf looked at Chance with admiration. Perhaps she *was* a next-generation Sherlock Holmes after all.

Clearly, Chance picked up on all these cues as well. She marched over to Gleb and ran her radiation detector up and down, sweeping him. She then did the same thing to Yefim. Wolf was not surprised when she said, "Wolf, Aar, please take Gleb into custody."

Gleb did not seem any more surprised than Wolf. "My family," he muttered before falling silent.

Chance explained the rest of the plan. "While you take Gleb to the brig, I'm going to check out the rest of the mansion here. See if I can find the polonium." She raised an eyebrow at Gleb. "I don't suppose you'd be willing to tell us where it is?"

Gleb sighed. "I flushed it down the toilet."

Chance pulled out her cell phone and called someone. "There's polonium in our waste disposal system. Is there any chance it will get recycled into our food production chain?" She paused, listening. "Well, you'll want to make sure, just in case." She slipped the phone back in her pocket. "As I was saying, I'm going to check out the rest of the mansion." She turned once more to Gleb. "And I'll see you in mediation," she said cheerfully. Her expression turned grim. "Hopefully Dmitri will be able to join us."

As Joshua tapped his wooden block on the desk to start the proceedings, he felt an enhanced appreciation of the movie "Lion King." The great Circle of Life had entered his mediation room. The leader of the attackers in his last violent crime case was now the victim.

As usual, he started by considering the victim. "Dmitri. Believe it or not, I'm sorry to see you like this." Dmitri sat in an oversized wheelchair, connected to what looked like half the plumbing of the BrainTrust, wheezing as he tried to breathe. Joshua turned to Dash, who stood next to Dmitri. "Is he going to be OK?"

Dash spoke cautiously. "I am hopeful. There are indications that his condition has reached bottom and he will improve from here."

Chance, standing on the other side of Dmitri, was fiddling with the controls. "Dmitri insisted on coming here today, but it would be best if we took him back to medical sooner rather than later."

Joshua nodded. "I'll see what I can do." He turned to Gleb. "I have determined that you, like most of the assailants in these cases, have no hope of paying anything like reasonable compensation to your victim." Really, Joshua was fascinated that in all these cases involving Dash and her friends, none of the defendants ever disputed the charges. He personally still had some doubts as to who should have been blamed when that Pakistani boy attacked Ping while she was dressed as a hooker, but as a mediator, it was as open and shut as a case could get. "Ordinarily in a situation like this, I would simply send you back to Russia."

Dmitri caught Joshua's eye, shaking his head vigorously. In disagreement. He turned and whispered to Chance. Chance turned to Joshua. "He says you can't send them back to Russia. It would be a death sentence."

Joshua wondered if he would ever really get used to having the victims defend their attackers. At least he was getting better at keeping the astonishment from interfering with his studiously objective mediator's face.

Now Gleb shook his head as vigorously as Dmitri had shaken his. "You *have* to send me back to Russia. You must."

OK, now that was a new wrinkle—the assailant refusing the victim's help, even though his life was on the line. Joshua couldn't help it; he lost control. The astonishment made him stare open-mouthed. "Are you telling me that you will *not* be executed upon arriving in Russia?"

Gleb stared away into a bleak distance only he could see. "That's not what I'm saying at all." Silence hung in the room. Finally, Gleb spoke again. "Mediator, sir, could I speak with you for a moment in private?"

Dmitri flailed in his chair. Chance leaned over to calm him and listened to him whisper once more, then told the room, "Whatever Gleb has to say, Dmitri wants to hear it." Dmitri nudged her. "He sort of demands it, actually."

Joshua put his face in his hands, then looked back up at Gleb beseechingly. "Well?"

Gleb frowned in exasperation. "As you wish, Mediator."

So Joshua retired to his private chambers with Gleb in

tow. Dmitri followed, with Dash and Chance in atten-
dance since they insisted that Dmitri not go anywhere
without them, especially not to a place where the assassin
would be, no matter that he was cuffed and chained and
stripped of anything that could possibly cause harm. As a
consequence, everybody from the main mediation room
was now crammed into his office. Too late, he realized
that he should have simply shut off the recording systems
in the main room. Well, perhaps the cramped, stuffy
quarters would inspire haste. Joshua addressed
Gleb. "Well?"

Gleb looked around at all the participants, and for a
moment Joshua feared he would refuse to speak. But in the
end he muttered, "I have to go back or the Premier will
execute my wife and daughter."

Dmitri thrashed once again. More whispering, and
Chance exclaimed, "You have a family? They're still in
Russia? Why didn't I know this?"

Gleb shrugged. "The Premier doctored the records. He
didn't want you to know. I didn't dare tell you."

Joshua stood up and backed away until his back was
against his bookshelves; his comforting books. "So if I send
you back he'll kill you, but if I don't send you back he'll kill
your family."

Dash spoke, the dark anger once more clouding her
eyes for a moment. "That man must be...stopped."

Chance spoke for Dmitri again. "You can't send
him back."

Gleb responded in terror, "You *have* to send me back."

Joshua waved his arms, driving everyone out. "Leave
me. I must think about this."

Joshua sat down at his desk, placed his face in his hands once more, and tried to figure out a solution.

In the end, he came up with a temporary fix. Amanda, the current chairman of the BrainTrust, was going to be furious with him. He could hardly wait to tell her. He returned to the main room and sat down. "I have made my decision." He gave everyone a wry smile, and you could have heard a pin drop. "Gleb shall be placed in the brig, in preparation for deportation to Russia—" as the entire victim's side of the room began to object he held up a finger sternly, "at a time of my selection, as yet to be determined."

Silence once again reigned as everyone in the room pondered the consequences.

The first person to react to this was Gleb. He collapsed into his chair with a sigh of relief. He realized, as Joshua had deduced, that the Premier would not execute his family while they could still be useful for leverage.

Dmitri was next. Chance offered, "Dmitri will happily pay the costs of keeping him in the brig indefinitely, and as promised during the last mediation, will also pay compensation to the victims as you see fit."

Ah, yes, Joshua remembered, Dmitri was on the hook for any bad behavior by his bodyguards. Of course, since the only person who needed to receive compensation in this case was Dmitri himself, it seemed a bit ludicrous. And inefficient. But he supposed he was glad to know that Dmitri was willing to fulfill his earlier promise. "Actually, Dmitri, I have a task for you when you're feeling better. Think of it as compensation for the victims."

Dmitri looked forlorn.

Joshua laughed. "Don't worry. It's a task for which you are uniquely qualified, and you'll even make a profit."

This caused Dmitri to raise an eyebrow, about as close as he could get to displaying eager anticipation in his current condition.

Joshua was not surprised when Dash brought up the complications in his solution. "Mediator Joshua, is my understanding incorrect? I thought the brig space on the BrainTrust was very limited and we could not have long-term prisoners."

Joshua waved his hands. "What else can I do? Do you have a proposal?" For just a moment, a bit of hope rose in his heart. Of all of them, Dash was the most likely to actually come up with a better solution.

Dash frowned. "I don't have a thought offhand. What is Amanda going to say about this?"

Joshua shuddered in half-mocking dread. "Since the very first day of BrainTrust operations, it has been an absolute policy to never have long-term prisoners aboard. I expect her to go through the roof," he paused, "before conceding that this is what we have to do."

Dash's eyes widened, and she held up her hand. "I just had a thought. What would Colin do? I have asked myself this question, and I believe I have an answer." She pulled out her phone. "You still need to put Gleb in the brig indefinitely, but perhaps we can make it a shorter indefinite period rather than a longer one." She hesitated, looked at her phone, and reluctantly put it back in her pocket. "My first idea is incomplete. I will need to think about this."

PRINCELINGS OF THE BLOOD

If you want ten years of prosperity, grow trees. If you want a hundred years of prosperity, educate children.
—Confucius

Lenora studied Qi Ru in puzzlement. "Let me get this straight. You snuck from the rural village where you grew up into Shanghai to try to get into college. When they discovered that you were *hukou*, which was not difficult because of the way you talk and the way you dress, in addition to the government's dossier on you, they rejected you, and sent you home, where everyone in your village laughed at you. So then you worked on a freighter to travel to Britain, and then worked your way through Oxford. You then got a job in high finance, and were on your way to achieving considerable success when you heard that a new BrainTrust archipelago was going to set up off the coast of China specifically to try to collect the best and brightest minds of the hinterlands in Western China, where there are no opportunities because of the caste system imposed by Mao almost a century ago. Upon hearing that we would be here soon, you flew back to China and chartered a ship to bring you out here, assuming we'd let you start a—what did you call it—a venture-capital matchmaking business?—even though you probably won't make anywhere near as much as you were making back in Britain as a derivatives trader."

Qi Ru nodded. "You have that mostly right. Technically, I worked as a derivatives trader in Edinburgh, Scotland, not in Britain. Most of the big trading houses moved out of London ten or so years after Britain left the Union." He waved his hands in a dismissive gesture. "But I'm not worried about making money here. I understand the plan. In exchange for free room, board, and education, the students here will offer a percentage of the value of all their inventions. Working with a lot of them on a lot of inventions, I expect to make a lot of money." He smiled wryly. "Perhaps not as much as I would have made in derivatives, but with the things we create here, we'll actually be able to see how our new creations impact people's lives and make them better." He cocked his head. "I figure that's worth a percentage."

Lenora looked at him thoughtfully. She could not think of a single thing wrong with bringing him directly onto the archipelago. He had already demonstrated both the intellectual strength and determination to qualify for a berth. And since he was arriving with substantial funds to invest, they'd have welcomed him on the BrainTrust itself with little review. But she would still test him. As much to test her testing process as to actually test him, she realized.

So she explained about the experiment she needed him to help her with before she tested him, and the voltage dial, and the electrical charges to be used to jolt the subject for better learning.

Qi Ru's eyes widened in amazement. "So you're using the Milgram experiment to separate good candidates from bad? I'm surprised anybody at all from China can pass the test. To pass, you have to refuse to electrocute a man to death while a scientist looks over your shoulder demanding obedience, right?"

Now Lenora's eyes widened. She began to laugh. "Yes, we are doing a variation of the Milgram experiment here, but it's not as bad as you think. We don't throw you off the boat just because you obey the authority figure— scientist —to the bitter end. And of course, the original Milgram experiment was much harder to interpret than Milgram fully appreciated at the time. A person who passed the test one day might fail utterly the next day, for example. But we collect enough data from the sensors in the chair and the cameras in the room, with facial micro-expressions and pupil dilations as the experiment progresses, that we can learn a great deal about the candidate's empathy, capacity for bonding, capacity for teamwork, ability to challenge authority, meta-thinking, and other important traits associated with success. It's critically valuable."

Qi Ru grunted. "It borders very close to torture for any honorable people you put through it. I'm surprised it's legal."

Lenora shook her head. "Well, it's not quite *il*legal, but it's generally considered unethical according to Western rules and regulations. They'd never license me as a psychologist or psychiatrist after this in the United States. Can't say I'd blame them." She shrugged. "Regardless, you've invalidated the test, which is one of the ways of passing. Congratulations, you're good to go."

"I'm still surprised that anybody from Western China ever passes."

Again Lenora shook her head. "Like I said, you don't fail just because you obeyed directions. You have to do really badly by all the measures taken by our analytical instruments to be rejected just on the basis of this test. But if you do badly enough—if you're a sociopath—you are definitely off the boat." She closed her eyes and grimaced. "Unless there is a very compelling reason to let you stay."

Guang Jiang peered at the simple control panel—the voltage dial and the charge button. He pointed down at the dial. "What's it mean when it goes into the red?"

Capt. Ainsworth fiddled with the buttons on his lab coat. The coat may have been a perfectly proper fit by some scientist's standards, but to him it felt bulky and ill-shaped. "From there, at the red line, as the voltage goes up it becomes increasingly dangerous for the subject." He realized Lenora was saying something else in his ear, so he must not have said the right thing. Whoops.

Guang nodded. "And the subject, he's just a worker, correct?"

This time the captain waited to hear what Lenora whispered in his ear. "He's a member of the BrainTrust."

Guang shrugged. "Are we ready?"

Once again the subject started the testing well, then got more and more wrong answers as the experiment proceeded. Guang dutifully raised the voltage again and again. He came into the red line and kept on going without an eyeblink. He came to the point where the subject ceased responding...and kept going. Finally, he pinned the dial against the maximum voltage setting and pressed the button one last time. "Well, that's that. Are we done?"

Lenora was whispering quite urgently into his ear, but the captain barely heard her. "You just killed the subject." He was pleasantly surprised that he said it softly rather than screaming.

Guang shrugged again. "He was just a worker. I assume you have many more." He stood up. "Anything else you'd like me to help you with before we start my testing?"

Jack spluttered, then said calmly, "No, thank you." As soon as Guang had left the room, Jack collapsed into the chair. "Psycho killer," he muttered.

Lenora had entered the room just in time to hear this comment. "Princelings," she said darkly. "Well, after that, we shouldn't have any surprises more unpleasant than what we've just seen."

"You have to find somebody besides me to do this."

Lenora visibly shook herself into a happier state, and responded with a chipper note to her voice, "Just two more to go!" She paused. "Two more and you're done."

The captain groaned.

Chen stepped up next. His eyes darted feverishly from side to side as he entered the room, as if expecting an attack at any moment from any corner. Having convinced himself that the place was safe, he turned his attention to the scientist, focusing on him with extreme concentration.

The captain explained the rules. Chen sat swiftly before the control panel, and the game began anew.

This game ended with sudden swiftness. When Chen Ying was first ordered to start the shocks he hesitated, and his hesitations became longer and more stressed as the shocks went higher. But suddenly the anxiety cleared from his face, and he started just pressing the button. When he was required to push the dial into the red zone, he turned to watch the captain's face as he brought his finger to rest on the activation key.

Whatever he saw caused him to move with swift confidence. He spun the dial to the far stop at the top end of the red zone and smashed the firing button without stopping. He smiled at the captain, whose careful mask of scientific scrutiny slipped away in horror. Chen stood up and went to the window. He tapped on it, then knocked harder. "Hey, man, get up! The test is over." Chen grunted a laugh and looked back at the captain. "This is all fake," he asserted. "You Westerners are such wimps that you'd never torture somebody for real." A mischievous brightness entered his eyes. "You just weren't upset enough when I started cooking that guy."

The captain stood frozen until Lenora entered the room, laughing. "You win, Chen. Sort of, anyway." She nodded to the door. "There's a bot out there that will lead you to your friends." She turned to the captain. "Buck up! We only have one more of these spoiled elitist princelings to go. Hopefully, we've run out of ways the test can go wrong."

Fan Hui ran the brush through her long silky hair one last time and walked with perfect composure into the testing room. A man wearing a white lab coat stood there, a tablet in one hand and a notation stylus in the other. She looked to him imperiously.

"All you have to do is follow the rules," the scientist said. He then went on to explain the educational process they were about to use together on the subject behind the window.

Fan Hui demanded, "So, is the subject a member of the BrainTrust, or is he someone you brought just for this testing?"

The scientist looked bemused. "Oh, he's a member of the Fuxing, all right."

"Ah. I am ready to proceed." Fan sat down in front of the control panel and placed one hand on the electrocution button, the other on the dial.

The questions began, and the right answers, and the wrong answers. Fan dutifully and methodically raised the voltage with each wrong answer, disregarding all forms of screaming and pleading from the person on the far side of the window.

Until the voltage reached the red line. After the subject

stopped begging and gave the wrong answer, Fan removed her hands from the control board and turned to the scientist. "We are done here," she asserted.

The scientist glared at her. "We are not done with the experiment."

Fan glared back with as much authority as the captain. "No. My father taught me to never waste my resources." She pointed through the window at the man slumped in the electric chair. "As a member of the Fuxing, he is one of my resources. I shall not waste him on a frivolous experiment."

The scientist pocketed his stylus. "Then you are correct. We are indeed done here."

"Excellent. Now that I have done this for you, we can begin my testing..." She paused as she started for the door. "Oh, wait. This was part of my testing, wasn't it?" A glimmer of appreciation appeared in her eyes. "Marvelous." She opened the door and stepped out, closely followed by the scientist. Lenora, Ciara, and Jam stood there talking. She spoke directly to Lenora. She spoke excitedly. "You've already taught me something very exciting." She pointed back at the room. "This test has just wonderful applications for my country."

Lenora blinked at her. Ciara said with suspicion, "applications? Like what?"

Fan explained, "So, there are two different outcomes that represent passing the test, depending on whether you are a member of the elite or of the peasantry." She looked away as she ordered her thoughts. "Members of the elite need to pass the test by refusing to destroy their asset, as I did. Peasants, on the other hand, must pass the test by obeying authority absolutely." She nodded pensively, more to herself than to the others in the room. "We can use this test to identify troublemakers and rebel leaders early. If we execute them as children, we can assure stability throughout the nation." She pulled her phone from her hip pocket. "I must tell my father. We can start conducting tests and executions on a demonstration basis in, say, Qinghai province, where we've been having trouble with rebellious peasants on a regular basis."

Ciara uttered a strangled gasp. "You can't be serious."

Fan looked up from her phone. "Why not?" she asked, truly puzzled.

Lenora spoke, bringing her own authority into play. "Before you do any testing or executions, there's a great deal more about this experiment that you need to understand before you can produce effective results. I strongly recommend you hold off on your...experiments...until your education has moved farther. Fan, you need to have a deeper understanding of the possibilities. Trust me, if you charge forward with your current very limited knowledge, you will execute the wrong people, and rue the side-effects you don't yet appreciate."

Fan frowned, clearly debating the merits of waiting versus the excitement of getting started immediately. "Very well. We can hold off a couple of months. Still, I must tell my father what an exciting first day I'm having." Then she nodded to the leaders of the archipelago, much as a corporate executive might acknowledge a group of underlings, before wandering down the passage, her head swaying as she worked the phone.

Jam spoke grimly. "And I thought Guang was going to be the main problem."

Lenora watched Fan disappear in the distance. A gleam entered her eyes, the gleam of a fighter entering the ring against a tough but beatable opponent. "Oh, I'm optimistic about Fan Hui."

Jack jerked at the buttons on his lab coat and tore it from his body. "Optimistic? You barely stopped her from running off to commit mass murder!"

Ciara's eyes watched her mother's face for a moment, then a smile caught the edges of Ciara's mouth. "Game theory."

Her mother looked back at her and gave her the acknowledging smile of a teacher looking upon a student who had just gotten a perfect score. "Game theory," she agreed. "And a teachable moment. I think she's gonna love game theory, so that part's easy." She frowned. "Though I'm not at all sure how we can arrange the teachable moment. That will require either wonderful luck or very careful planning."

Meanwhile, the captain slumped against the wall. "You need to find someone else to be your pseudo-scientist," he demanded. "I can't do this anymore. Can't you just make me navigate the fleet through a typhoon or something else easy the next time?"

Lenora chuckled. "You are relieved of duty. I have an idea for your replacement anyway. Patriarchy or not, I'm thinking that with a little training, Fan herself might be quite good as the scientist."

The captain goggled at her for a moment, then left the room without comment.

Two days later, Lenora called the captain. "I'd like to hold a meeting in your conference room, up off the bridge."

"Sounds mysterious, Lenora. Why not just use your own conference room? Heaven knows, it's a lot more comfortable than mine."

Lenora answered, "Because this is ship's business, not mission business, and I want us all to understand how serious it is. My conference room is designed to make the participants comfortable, just as you said. Yours, on the other hand, is so austere, it forces the attendees to stare at hard decisions realistically. We all need to be alert to the consequences as we make this decision."

So Fleet Captain Ainsworth, Security Chief Baddeley, Expeditionary Leader Jam, and Mission Commander Thornhill gathered in the captain's conference room. After they sat down, the captain turned to Lenora. "Your meeting. What's the topic?"

Lenora folded her hands on the tabletop and stared at them. "We have to talk about Fan and Guang." She looked around the room. "The other princeling, Chen, performed with excellence. He'd actually qualify for a full-ride scholarship, not that we're going to give it to him. I'd be delighted to have him even if he didn't confer to us the advantage of having powerful parents who now have an incentive to help us."

Jam leaned forward and spoke with warm anger. "Guang tells the story of electrocuting his subject quite proudly. A psychopath. A source of endless trouble. Why is this even a discussion? Get him off the boat."

Lenora sighed. "I wish it were that simple. One problem is that our strategy of accepting the children of high-ranking members of government is a two-edged sword. Guang has already been kicked out of more than one college. We are, in some sense, his last hope. If we keep him, his parents will be tremendously grateful. But if we reject him, we will acquire a powerful enemy. A terribly powerful enemy."

Jam continued to argue. "Still, you've already said we're acquiring powerful friends through Chen. Surely we can lose this one."

The captain shook his head. "They don't compare. Chen's mom is in the Politburo. But Guang's father..."

Hart continued in disgust, "He's on the Standing Committee. The top of the top. He could order the execution of Chen's family and no one would say a word."

Lenora shifted the topic. "And on top of that, and even more important from my personal perspective, his girl-friend Fan is a gem." She looked up at the ceiling. "Well, a gem with some ethics problems I think we can fix, but a gem nonetheless. She could easily be the one who makes this archipelago a success. But she's very attached to her boyfriend. She left Oxford just to be with him when they kicked him out."

Jam pressed her lips together. "So we're stuck with him? What if he does something really vile? Do we know why he got kicked out of his last university? Because we need to be ready." She glared around the room. "We need to be able to kick him out later if he becomes enough of a problem."

Hart assented. "I can pound on him some if he gets a

little out of hand, but from what I've heard he's not very good at learning, even when hit with a baseball bat."

Lenora nodded. "Yes, we can kick him off if he gets bad enough. We'll take our chances with his father if we have to." She paused pensively. "And maybe we can arrange for Fan to realize just what a dud he is before we do it."

JEWEL IN THE SKY

If a prediction for the future sounds like science fiction, it is probably wrong. If it does not sound like science fiction, it is certainly wrong.
   —Chris Peterson, Foresight Institute

Equipped with its new complement of four hundred Quantum Zero Speed gyroscopic stabilizers, the *Heinlein* had sailed beyond the confines of the BrainTrust reef into the not-quite-so-calm waters beyond. The goal had been to move far enough away so the BrainTrust would be safe in the event of an accident. For this goal, they had only been partly successful. The *Heinlein* might have left the Brain-Trust behind, but not quite all of the BrainTrust had left the *Heinlein*. Two ships, the *Haven* and the *Argus*, had followed her beyond the reef.

Matt was not amused. "You're still too damned close," he complained.

Dmitri slapped him on the shoulder hard enough to

knock down anyone but an ex-football player. "Nonsense! Why, you let crowds of onlookers closer than this at Cape Canaveral for your launches."

They stood on the immense balcony outside Dmitri's immense bay window separating his immense living room from inclement weather on the *Haven*. Gina snuggled against her husband on the right, her hand wrapped around his upper arm. Dmitri stood to his left.

A freezing wind off the ocean should have made the balcony uninhabitable, but a series of huge infrared lamps and a beautiful green-glazed fire pit kept it toasty despite the chill. A handful of other guests stood in another cluster, looking out at the towering multicolor jewel that was the first Kestrel Titan rocket.

The other cluster stood protectively around Dash, who had wrapped her traditional lab coat around her like armor, as if expecting another kidnapping attempt at any moment. The people with her seemed to expect it as well. At least, everyone except Chance expected it. She had recovered from the kidnapping ordeal with remarkable speed, and had even greeted Yefim with hearty good cheer when they arrived. Yefim had tried to kidnap them and Chance had given him a concussion for his efforts, so they were square.

Chance, Toni, Amanda, Lindsey, and Ben hovered close enough that Dash welcomed the occasional gust of wind that brought her a cool breath of fresh oxygen. Yefim stood in a corner of the living room off the balcony, his shoulders hunched as if he were still trying to apologize for the recent debacle.

This gathering was both smaller and less formal than

the last party for a rocket launch. It was a shame they had so few onlookers, because the rocket being launched was a work of art. Since she was built with titanium, it had been a simple matter to stress the surface in such a manner that it shone with an iridescent swirl of colors like titanium jewelry...and like the superstructure of the *Elysian Fields*, the tourist isle ship for which some BrainTrust engineers with more time than sense had perfected the stress-coloring technique.

Matt had been furious when he first saw his engineers creating a coloration test patch by one of the landing struts on the central core booster. He was terrified it would introduce structural weakness as a worst case and set them behind schedule even in the best case. But Colin had shown him on the PERT chart that the color stressing could be done in parallel without using any resources from the critical path. And Alex and Werner had all gently assured him it would not impair the rocket's function.

After half the work crew had come up to him and congratulated him on the boldness of his decision to make a rocket as beautiful as it was functional, Matt gave up and wrote it off as a price for employee morale.

Matt looked to the side to see the other ship that had sailed out here to watch the launch. Alex, Werner, and Colin waved at him from behind the plexiglass gunwale of the *Argus*. Matt cupped his hands around his mouth and shouted, "You're too close!"

Gina whispered in his ear, "Futile, even if they could hear."

Matt muttered, "No one listens to me anymore."

Gina laughed softly. "You picked them. Best and brightest."

Matt muttered back, "Does best and brightest have to mean least manageable and most obstreperous?"

Gina chuckled. "How could *you* not know?"

The countdown for the last ten seconds began.

The Premier stretched back on his black leather sofa in the living room of his Northern dacha, hands behind his head, watching the snowfall outside while he kept the corner of his eye on the *Heinlein* displayed on his wallscreen.

He loved watching the snow cover the world while he sat snug in his warm house. By now, the snow had covered the roads so thoroughly, this home could only be reached with snowshoes or cross-country skis. If the Apocalypse came and destroyed everything, he and Pascha would be among the handful of survivors.

And as it happened, a small apocalypse was about to arrive for the BrainTrust. The final countdown for the Kestrel Titan, so, so beautiful, had begun. He turned his full attention to watching its moment of life and its swift death.

The countdown finished, and the rocket's boosters came to life. Any moment now, his plan would come to fruition. The rocket lifted up, and up... And up, and up.

The Premier glared at the screen. Where was the mighty explosion he had paid for? What had happened to the virus whose insertion had been indisputably verified? What could possibly have gone wrong?

Matt groaned. "Screwed up."

Gina answered as she watched the rocket lift over their heads. "Over the BrainTrust?"

Matt's eyes followed hers. "You'd think we could have moved it a little further to the west. If something goes wrong now, the whole archipelago could go up in flames." His voice turned from mournful to sour. "Or maybe just the newer ships with magnesium superstructures."

Lindsey sidled up next to Dmitri. Speaking across the Russian, she asked, "Matt, is it supposed to be going straight over everyone's head?" Her eyes gleamed. "I may get a good story out of this, after all."

The Chief Advisor sat alone in the war room. The primary wallscreen was linked to a public broadcast of the Kestrel launch. The Advisor stared at the multicolored rocket in bewilderment. Why would you make a giant rocket look like a child's toy or a piece of cheap jewelry? Those people were lunatics.

A secondary screen showed the Combat Information Center on the *Vella Gulf* with the captain front and center. The Advisor knew he was pestering the captain, but he could not help himself. "And the troops are all ready to go? In case something happens, I mean."

The captain closed his eyes momentarily lest the Advisor see him roll his eyes in disgust. "Yes, sir everyone's ready here. And on the *Zumwalt* and *Harper's Ferry* as well."

"Excellent." The chief advisor dared not ask the captain about Seal Team 3 on board the *Zumwalt*. It would seem oddly specific, and the only people who knew the real mission were the fire team leaders of the Seal Team. Everyone else would actually try to help the survivors of the explosion. Only the Seal Team would actually engage in the critical search for Doctor Dash.

The final ten count came and went. The absurdly colorful Kestrel Titan, looking like a firework itself, lifted off. The Chief Advisor rose and walked to the wallscreen, bringing his nose practically to touch with the fiery rocket. He became even more excited as the rocket started to tilt over and race at ever accelerating velocity towards the BrainTrust. This was it...

The rocket soared over the BrainTrust. He tensed in anticipation of a crescendo of fire!

And then the rocket was beyond the floating ships, accelerating ever faster and higher into the heavens. The Chief Advisor gaped at the screen.

The captain of the *Vella Gulf* coughed to get his attention. "Sir, it looks like we won't be needed for rescue operations after all. Might it be reasonable to stand down at this point?"

For a long moment, the Chief Advisor stared unseeing and speechless. Finally, he growled, "Yes, yes, of course. Stand down. You can return the troops to their previous dispositions at your leisure."

"Thank you, sir," the captain offered respectfully.

The Chief Advisor grunted, then disconnected the cruiser captain from his secondary wallscreen.

What could have possibly gone wrong?

Matt barked at his cell phone, demanding an immediate connection with Werner. He watched from Dmitri's balcony as Werner on the *Argus* lifted his phone to answer. Matt spoke swiftly. "Next time, we're launching from much farther from the archipelago. And to the southwest, for God's sake!"

Werner was too happy to pay much attention to Matt's anger. "Of course, of course. We only kept the *Heinlein* close for this launch in case we needed to get emergency crews out there quickly."

Matt covered his eyes with his hand. "Fine. I'll be over in a few minutes." Pocketing his phone, he saw Dash approach with her coterie out of the corner of his eye. He turned to her, forcing himself to smile.

Dash smiled back brightly. "That was a beautiful launch. And especially let me compliment you on how beautiful the rocket itself is. Transforming it into a piece of titanium jewelry was a brilliant stroke of creativity."

Matt stood speechless. Gina nudged him and spoke on his behalf. "Don't you think so? Everyone loves what he did with it. I have to concede it was one of his more brilliant ideas."

Matt glared at his wife for a moment, then broke down in laughter. "Yeah, I thought it was pretty clever, but just to be clear, it wasn't my idea. The real credit goes to Alex. Or Werner. Or my entire workforce, depending on who you ask."

Dash nodded. "Well, you still deserve the credit for allowing them free rein. It's not every boss who has the wisdom to let his people go a little crazy with a good idea every now and then."

Gina nudged Matt again and answered smugly, "Exactly what I've been telling him."

The rocket had disappeared into the distance. As Werner walked back inside the *Argus*, he remembered something he'd been wanting to ask. "Colin, I've been wondering about some lost software code on these new chips from the BrainTrust."

He stopped walking a little ways inside the passageway before they reached the promenade. Here the walls showed displays of an island paradise with palm trees and a pirate ship off the coast as several children flew overhead. Captain Hook shook his fist at them.

Colin stopped next to Werner. "Lost software? Sounds serious. What happened?"

Werner shook his head. "My software release manager uploaded a series of enhancements to the computers on the Kestrel Titan days ago. As per standard procedure, he downloaded the result and confirmed that the upgrade had been completed successfully. But when he went to make another upload the following day, the earlier changes weren't there anymore. So he reentered them, and when he checked for them yet again the following day they were still there, so they seem to have stuck the second time. But it's still worrisome."

"Ah." Colin nodded knowingly. "Your production manager probably entered his authorization code incorrectly the first time and got his update trapped in our security honeypot."

Werner shook his head, not understanding. "A security honeypot?"

"Of course. Surely someone has mentioned that the main buyers of BrainTrust chips are people with deep concerns about privacy. So when someone uses an invalid authorization to enter the system, if the intruder attempts to insert code or data, his insertion is directed into a virtual machine tied to his access code so that anytime he and his associates break into the system they see their own hacked version."

Alex chimed in, "That's why it's called a honeypot. The attackers are lured in and can't leave."

Colin nodded. "Since he can see he succeeded, the attacker is less likely to try again. Of course, the actual chip, its code, and its execution are all unaffected by this. As a systems administrator and owner of the chip, there's a way to access, read out, and purge these hacker-trapping virtual machines, so you can see what the attackers have attempted to do."

Werner sighed. "Hardly seems relevant to us. It's not like anybody would want to read or infect our controller chips."

Colin hesitated as if he might object, but in the end, he just shrugged. "In any event, inspecting the attack code doesn't make sense for anyone except those who are under assault from the most dedicated of professional cyber attackers." He pulled out his phone. "Shall I text the lead engineer in charge of the honeypots, and have him send someone over to help you purge the chips? There's no real danger leaving them alone, but you might want to delete them just to keep your systems clean."

Werner shrugged. "Sure." As Colin texted, Werner grumbled, "We wouldn't have had this problem if we'd just been able to use our own chips. Blasted California government, confiscating our shipment like that. How'd they even know those chips were ours? They weren't even addressed to us. Keenan Stull at Goldman Sachs was taking the delivery. Damnable luck."

Now Colin's eyes brimmed with unexplained mirth. "Indeed. Lady Luck makes a fickle and uncertain partner. Best not to have her on the team at all." As Werner moved off, Colin muttered under his breath, "Far, far better, to have someone more reliable than the Lady to make your luck. A skill all project directors should cultivate."

Werner turned to him. "What's that?"

Colin smiled brightly. "Coming," he said, lengthening his stride to catch up.

Two days later Dash found herself getting off the elevator on the Babylon deck of the *GS Prime*. It was her first visit to the Goldman Sachs isle ship. Keenan Stull was throwing a small party of his own for Matt and SpaceR.

Dash had no idea why she had been invited, but it seemed that partying had become much more commonplace on the BrainTrust since the arrival of the *Haven* and SpaceR. Perhaps things would settle down now with the Titan operational. She certainly hoped so. She had work to do.

Heading for the party's conference room, passing Babylon's Hanging Gardens, she found Matt bent over, studying some detail of the passageway artwork. Dash looked over his shoulder.

A massive ziggurat rose into the clouds. She could see the column continued above the clouds, off to infinity. She realized that this must be the Tower of Babel, man's most arrogant attempt to reach Heaven and be as God.

A detail caught her attention, and she found herself bent over just like Matt, scrutinizing the workers with tools traveling up and down the spiral path around the column. Each person wore an earbud wired to a cell phone at the hip.

In the Goldman Sachs version of the story, after God struck men down and made them speak different languages so they could no longer work together, the people had developed translator apps and finished the job. She peered up again and saw the people on the path above the clouds carried not tools but suitcases. Travelers to Heaven. Mission accomplished.

Matt muttered, more for himself than for her, "Elisabeth."

"What?" Dash asked.

"The artist who created this." He stood up. "I'll need something like this for the *Helios*—the new SpaceR manufacturing ship we're building so we can stop sharing the *Argus* with the BrainTrust. SpaceR deserves a deck theme like this at least as much as these people."

Dash made the obvious recommendation. "Ask Colin who she is. He probably knows."

Matt nodded thoughtfully and held out his arm. "May I escort you to the party? Gina's going to be late."

Dash took his arm. "Didn't we already celebrate the success of the Kestrel Titan? Do we really need another party?"

Matt laughed. "Oh, we're not celebrating the launch. Old news. No, as of today, SpaceR has moved everyone and everything of value out of California. What we're celebrating is California's achievement."

Dash looked at him in puzzlement. "Achievement?"

Matt smiled triumphantly. "Oh, yes. The governor is finally getting his fair share."

AUTHOR'S NOTES

Author: Readers, I'm delighted to inform you that the main characters of the BrainTrust have agreed to an interview. Here they are: Ping, Jam, and of course Dr. Dyah Ambarawati.

Dash: You know better. It's not like we're strangers. Call me Dash.

Author: Of course. I got a little confused there. Stage fright.

Ping: So, book two is done, right? When do we celebrate?

Author: As soon as we're done with this interview.

Ping: Cool. What do you want to know?

Author: Well, normally I go through and talk about the reality behind all the different forms of tech used in the story. For example, Dash, what about the stealth mode created for Jam's copters?

Dash: Of course that's real. They were doing successful

experiments back in 2017 to absorb radar waves with graphene. It was just lab work in those days, of course.

Jam: What copters?

Dash: Uh, you know Jam doesn't even learn about the copters till book three, right? Ted and I are still fleshing out the details.

Author: Oops. Let's move on quickly then. What about the Graphene Reinforced Carbon used for the launch pad on the *Heinlein*?

Dash: That wasn't developed until much later. It seems like an obvious extension of the principles of carbon-fiber-reinforced carbon, though.

Author: Of course. But really, the big tech used in this book is the Accel educational software framework. Is there anything like that in reality?

Dash: No. Of course, scientists have been researching adaptive learning and testing since the Seventies. For example, with adaptive presentation of increasingly harder questions, you can assess a student's competence with fewer than ten questions as accurately as you could with a standard hundred-question test. Adaptive learning can similarly zoom in on the student's particular challenges, spending the student's time exactly where needed, enabling much faster movement through the material.

Author: So, it works much the same way the optometrist gives you an eye exam?

Dash: Very much so. But none of it has penetrated the public school systems. There's nothing like Accel. I'm deeply puzzled by that, actually. Why *isn't* there anything like Accel?

Author: One problem is that adaptive learning is

wicked hard to program. The tools aren't really ready. But even so, you'd have expected more progress in deployed systems if you had a competitive market. Alas, there's little competitive about Western education. Certainly, the textbook publishers would lobby against a system like Accel that cuts out the middleman. And surely the state regulators who certify educational materials would oppose something that continuously improved itself. How could they certify it when it was going to get better the next day? And a lot of open-source educational software developers would rail against the idea of letting module authors profit from their efforts.

Dash: But…any decent introductory text on incentive engineering would show how valuable money is as one of a suite of rewards. If you want to enhance the reliability with which higher quality materials are produced, you should really include money. Incentive engineering—it's a crucial idea.

Author: Dash, let me remind you. We're in 2018 now. There is no field of incentive engineering yet.

Dash: Oh. Forgot. Incentive engineering as a discipline won't exist until—

Author: Stop right there. Remember the rules. You can't be telling the readers about the actual future.

Jam: Could I ask a question?

Author: Of course. Though I may not be able to answer, you understand.

Jam: What are we going to do about the Chief Advisor and the Premier? I mean, they keep giving us trouble.

Ping: Yeah, when do we get to whack 'em?

Author: I, uh. Ahem. So, I think it's pretty clear what's

going to happen to the Chief Advisor, eventually. The Premier's case is more complicated.

Ping: So we don't get to whack 'em? What about Fan Hui? We've really got to whack her.

Author: You seem to have an awful lot of heartburn with someone who hasn't actually done anything awful yet. You seem to know her. Anything you want to tell me about that?

Ping: As you know better than anyone, I lived most of my life in Chicago.

Jam: I have a request. Could you please give Joshua a break?

Dash: Give Joshua a break? From what?

Ping: He really does like us despite the way we treat him, you know.

Dash: What's wrong with the way we treat him?

Author: He likes you? Are you sure?

Ping: Of course. We talk with him in between chapters. What do you think we do between chapters, sleep?

Author: I hadn't really thought about it.

Ping: Am I ever going to get to use my Big Gun, or are you going to keep teasing me with it forever?

Author: I probably shouldn't tell you this, but...you should keep practicing with it.

Ping: Really?

Author: Upside down.

Ping: Upside... What?

Jam: I wanted to thank you for bringing Captain Ainsworth and Security Chief Hart back. It was so great to see them again! You treated them like such minor characters in the first book. You didn't even give them real names. How'd they wind up in book two?

Author: Funny story. The narrator for the Harmony of Enemies audiobook gave them such wonderful British accents, I couldn't resist. So I promoted them, asked them for their names, and the rest is history. Future history, that is.

Ping: Upside-*what*?

Jam: Could you give us any hints about who we're going to fight in the future? A couple books from now? I guess our plate is already pretty full for book three.

Author: There's a new character. He's...really scary. As smart as Dash. I'm glad he's confined to the pages of the book.

Ping: Let me guess—you won't let me just whack him now.

Author: Couldn't even if I wanted to. You're all invulnerable except when you're in a scene, for which you should be thankful. He knows you already, knows the threat you represent, and his assassins are as scary as he is. They bring a kind of trouble you have not yet known.

Ping: Bring 'em.

Dash: I too have a request.

Author: Of course. Anything within my power.

Dash: I was really upset when you pushed me into a situation where we all got a glimpse of my dark side. I didn't even know I *had* a dark side. I'm still very upset. Could you please not put me into any more situations where that comes up?

Author: I'm so sorry. You know that's not how this works. Sure, I set up the initial conditions, but after that, I just observe and tell the story. You guys are the ones who create it.

Dash: Which is just as it should be.

Jam: *Allahu Akbar.*

Ping: Hallelujah. I see they're bringing in the champagne. Can we celebrate now?

CONNECT

Join the BrainTrust discussion group on Facebook at

https://www.facebook.com/groups/326423271191445/

50588006R00162

Made in the USA
Columbia, SC
10 February 2019